ROD DAMON CAN'T MAKE LOVE! ARE HIS DAYS
AS A COXEMAN OVER?

Rod Damon—The Coxeman—uncovers a bizarre plot
to assassinate several world leaders. HECATE, the enemy
force, has planted remote-controlled "bugs" in the brains
of its agents—"bugs" which are programmed to make the
men kill on command.

Rod tries to join HECATE in the hope that he can
destroy it. After several unusual entrance exams—
including a test of his virility—Rod makes the grade as a
HECATE agent.

The Coxeman is "bugged" for murder.

But he *can't* neutralize the assassination plot.

And he *can't* make love—except on HECATE's orders.

What *can* he do?

Read on . . . and see for yourself!

COXEMAN #10

THE BEST LAID PLANS

AN ADULT NOVEL BY BY TROY CONWAY

POPULAR LIBRARY

Copyright © 1969 by Coronet Communication, Inc.
All rights reserved. Except as permitted under the U.S. Copyright Act of 1976, no part of this publication may be reproduced, distributed, or transmitted in any form or by any means, or stored in a database or retrieval system, without the prior written permission of the publisher.

Popular Library
Hachette Book Group USA
237 Park Avenue
New York, NY 10017

Popular Library is an imprint of Grand Central Publishing. The Popular Library name and logo is a trademark of Hachette Book Group USA, Inc. The Coxeman name and logo is a trademark of Hachette Book Group USA, Inc.

Visit our Web site at www.HachetteBookGroupUSA.com

First Printing: February 1969

Printed in the United States of America

Conway, Troy
Best Laid Plans, The / Troy Conway
(Coxeman, #10)

ISBN 0-446-54314-4 / 978-0-446-54314-9

CHAPTER ONE

The big red Buick was doing eighty miles an hour.

It was coming along Alumni Row, which fronts the University Memorial Union building, and it was like a scarlet bullet. I saw it and stopped at the crosswalk. Rhea Carson saw it and stopped beside me.

Rhea Carson is a lady diplomat, highly connected in the State Department. She is a very valuable person to the United States. She is the only person in our known world that the Arab States trust, and that the Israeli government also trusts. Abdel Nasser likes her, as do King Hussein of Jordan, Shah Mohammed Reza Palayi of Iran, King Faisal of Saudi Arabia, Houari Boumediene of Algeria, and the President of Syria, Noureddin Attassi. So, too, do Moyshe Dayan and Premier Levi Eshkol of Israel.

When the red car was a hundred feet away—

Rhea Carson leaped in front of it.

I had just turned to ask her a question. I had been selected by the Board of Trustees to escort Miss Carson around the university campus. She was here to make a speech in the new gymnasium that holds upwards of eighteen thousand people, this very evening. Not a vacant seat could be found for that address.

Her topic was to be: The Prospects of Permanent Peace Between Arabs and Israelis in the Near East. Not only university students were to be there, but members of the United Nations, some congressmen, and a couple of foreign ambassadors.

Rhea's work at the United Nations behind closed doors with members of the United Arab Republic, and behind closed doors with Israeli representatives, had brought the faint promise of hope to all Middle East negotiations. Instead of war, there might be peace. Her silver tongue, her

5

calm confidence, her liking for both Arab and Israeli as members of the brotherhood of men, were world famous.

She must live to continue that great beginning.

But now—

Rhea Carson was trying to commit suicide!

I did not stand there frozen. My name is Rod Damon, I am a sociology professor at the university. I am also the founder of the League for Sexual Dynamics, which I work with as an adjunct to the sociology program. Add in the facts that I do secret agent work for the Thaddeus X. Coxe Foundation and that I am trained to react with lightning speed to the new or unusual, and you may get some idea of why I did what I did so fast.

She was in mid-air when I jumped, diving at her the way a Green Bay flanker back dives for a runner. I went off my feet, my arms pincered in on the Carson hips, my head bent to ram her thigh with extra force.

The car was on top of us.

It was going to be a near thing, at best. My arms went around a pair of soft thirty-six-inch hips and locked tight. My momentum carried us both forward. I heard Rhea Carson give a shrill cry. Of dismay? Of despair? Of delight? I could not tell.

Something hit my ankle, spun me.

Then the lady diplomat was going down hard on the pavement of the road with me on top of her, and the red car was a scarlet blur out of the corners of my eyes. Rhea Carson bounced. I bounced right along with her. We lay there panting, staring into each other's eyes.

"What the hell were you trying to do?" I rasped.

Her green eyes filled with tears. Her red lower lip quivered. "I—I d-don't know. All of a sudden—I had to hurl myself in front of that car."

She sniffled and her body began to shake in nervous tremors. She lay gasping under me and her soft flesh moved and all I could think was, she felt damn good against my hard body.

I realized where we were and that students were running toward us across the campus. Hundreds of eyes were glued to our quivering bodies. I tried to smile down at her as I wriggled off her belly and got to my feet.

I caught her wrist and lifted her up.

"You all right, Professor?" a girl called.

"Like, man, that was a rare scare!" a boy howled.

"How about you, Mrs. Carson?"

She was smiling, brushing at her blouse and skirt, flushing a little, trying to be a good sport about the attention. I gave her a hand to dislodge some of the dirt adhering to her skirt. It was then I noticed she had no girdle on. Her buttocks were soft, smooth and they jiggled where I touched them.

"I—I'm all right," she told the students, blinking in her nervousness. My hand caught her elbow firmly.

"You're coming along with me, young lady," I said, turning her on a heel and helping her to the walk.

"Oh, but really! I don't want to be any bother," she said hurriedly.

I knew how to deal with women. It's a big part of my job. In my roles as professor and sexologist, I am in constant contact with girl students, lady teachers and administrators, female deans. Mostly, I can read them like a book.

Rhea Carson wanted to be pampered. She wanted a male to fuss over her, reassuring her against the fright that still etched lines on her face. But she could not come out openly and say so; she had to rely on my instinctive understanding.

"My hose, my face," she was saying, almost running as I hurried her along. "I must be a fright."

"My pad isn't far. A few minutes. It's just off campus, really. You can lie down and take a rest. I'll bring you Irish coffee, in the proper glass."

She laughed, half sobbing.

While I was lifting out the key to my apartment in the four-apartment house where I am a tenant, she began to cry. The tears just welled up in her eyes and trickled down her cheeks. It was her feminine reaction to her near-miss with death; I was damn glad it hadn't happened sooner. I could handle a hysterical female in my rooms, but on the street it might have been a different matter.

I pushed open the door; my hand at the small of her back pushed her forward into the living room of my little suite. She bent her head, let her face fall forward into her cupped hands, and bawled.

7

"I—I wanted to do it, I really wanted to kill myself," she sobbed. "The man in the car wasn't trying to kill me!" I had thought of that possibility, but now I discarded the notion completely. Her wet face raised to look at me. "I actually t-tried to c-commit suicide!"

"But that's silly. Why should you want to do that?"

"I d-don't know. That's what frightens me."

She was shaking all over in the first stages of incipient hysteria. I had to do something to snap her out of it, or she would become a hospital case. And with her talk due for eight o'clock tonight, this would be front page news stuff.

I guided her to an easy chair. "You sit down there. I'm going to make you comfortable."

As she sat, I knelt down and reached under her skirt, sliding my palms along her stockinged thighs. She forgot her tears and her fright and sat up a little straighter.

She said, "Oh!"

"I just want to take your stockings off, to check for bruises." I smiled up at her startled face. My fingers were working on the garterclasp, unfastening it and its two mates. I began rolling down the black nylon.

"But—but really. . . ."

Her thighskin was very smooth. Creamy. Was I mistaken, or did her leg give a little shiver where my fingertips caressed her? She did not push my hand away, but her color heightened.

I undid the other garter and rolled down the other stocking. With the nylons crumpled at her ankles, I slipped off her shoes and removed the stockings. Her legs were damn shapely, naked with her skirt hem pushed to her upper thighs.

She half laughed, "I'm showing you a lot, Professor."

I was putting her stockings in her shoes as I let my eyes assess her legs. I nodded, saying, "But you aren't worrying about what happened back there."

Her laughter rang out. It was nice laughter, a little deep and throaty. Cleopatra might have laughed like that, or Delilah, or even Jezebel. There is much of all those women in every female born.

I leaned forward and kissed her soft thigh, well above the knee. Her flesh smelled good, with the faintest trace of

Shalimar perfume. Up this close, I could see beneath the skirt hem to her black girdle. Rhea Carson wore no panties, so my eyes had a treat.

"Well, really," she gasped as her fingers caught my head and held it motionless. "I ought to feel insulted, Professor! What in the world do you think you're doing?"

Her voice told me with its quaver that she was not as averse to my kisses as her words implied. Her fingers were quivering on my head, but they did not move my lips away from her soft thighflesh. Rhea Carson was poised on a psychic fence. One wrong move and she would flop one way; the right move, even the right words, might topple her over on my side where the fun was, and where there was no incipient hysteria.

"You're a damn attractive female, Rhea," my lips told her, moving against her thighflesh. "I think you forget about that when you get so involved with the international situation."

My lips kissed along the soft thigh. The hands on my head went right along with me, as if they were mesmerized.

It would have been fatal to tell her I just wanted to get her mind off the near-accident. I would have insulted her femininity, which means: her appeal to a male. A woman can forgive almost anything but that. Rhea Carson was no exception, diplomat though she might be.

"I'm going to tell you something you can file away and then forget," I went on, still kissing up and down her shivering thigh. "When I saw you, I told myself you were one female I'd like to take to bed."

It was a risk. She could get to her feet and go storming out of my pad, assuring me she was going to make a complaint to the university authorities. I might get the sack for what I was doing, for what I'd just said. But if I knew my women—and as the founder of L.S.D. I flattered myself that I did—she would sit and take it, and silently beg for more. It had been a long time since Rhea Carson had thought of herself in terms of legs, breasts and her own latent sexuality.

Her eyes were mere slits, staring down at me. Her tonguetip was moistening her full red mouth. Almost for the first time, I looked at her as a possible bedmate.

9

She was in her late thirties, she was four inches over five feet, and she weighed in the neighborhood of a hundred and twenty pounds. This poundage was nicely distributed. Her hips were wide, her middle was slim, but she carried a pair of breasts that made big bulges in her tailored blouse. It may have been my imagination, but the bulges looked bigger than they had been before I took her stockings off.

"Better undress," I informed her happily. "Please stand."

"You must be j-joking! I haven't taken my clothes off in front of a man in five years." She was still poised on the borderline between hysteria and anger. Her eyes were wide, her full lips trembled. Shock had entered her system by this time, but I was giving her something beside her troubles to think about, and I could only hope it would work.

"You should have . . . lots of times," I told her, putting a palm on her calf and sliding it up to her soft outer thigh and back again. "You're a very attractive woman."

"I'm a woman with a curse," she whispered, her fear showing again. Under my hand her thigh trembled, but her libido had nothing to do with it.

I lifted to my feet. She made a pretty picture, seated on the big divan with her legs nude from upper thighs to her red toenails. I sat down beside her, put my left arm about her shoulders. She was going to require the gentle, slow approach. So I set about it, drawing her closer.

"Tell me," I breathed.

"I—I've tried to kill myself before this," she whimpered. Her head fell sideways onto my shoulder. Her eyelids closed.

"It was in a Paris hotel. I tried to throw myself out a window of the ninth floor. Luckily, the chambermaid opened the door just as I was sliding a leg over the sill. She caught me and dragged me back."

My right hand was stroking her cheek and throat. I let my palm slip downward so that it could feel the heaviness of her breast. She stirred a little, her thighs pressed together, she opened her lips to breathe. I was transferring one emotional spasm to another, and she didn't fight me.

10

"If you didn't have suicidal tendencies, you wouldn't have tried to kill yourself," I pointed out.

"But I never have had them," she whispered defensively. "I'm a happy woman. I have money, everything I want. I'm well thought of, everywhere."

"What about your husband? Could trouble with him cause you to have a death complex?"

Her nipples were getting hard under my hands. She was twisting a little to the sensations building in her flesh. I went on caressing her breasts.

She licked her lips while her head shook back and forth. "My husband died some years ago."

"Perhaps subconsciously you want to join him?"

"No. Nothing like that. We were never madly in love. He was in the diplomatic service too. We would go months on end without seeing each other."

I am an amateur psychologist, in connection with my sociology work, but her problem was too deep-rooted for me to find. All I could do was prevent hysteria until a psychiatrist took over.

When she began to cry again, softly, I drew her sideways and with my fingers under her chin, lifted her mouth to my kiss. I caught her lips between mine. I kissed her gently, wetly. Her body shivered, she pressed her mouth to mine and let her lips go wide.

Her lips were moist, her tongue was a silent voice calling out to me for help and reassurance. My own mouth and tongue gave her that reassurance while I used a finger and a thumb to draw down her blouse zipper. As she felt the cool air on her back, she let her breasts mash into my chest.

When she drew back for air, mouth open and her cheeks flushed, I drew her blouse off her shoulders and down her arms. Her plump shoulders were indented by blue brassiere straps, her milky breasts overflowed the bra cups in creamy softness that shook as she breathed.

I kissed her bared shoulders, I ran my mouth down to the swells of her breasts where they bulged up out of the C cups. My tongue ran across that warm breastflesh where it was exposed.

"I must be crazy," she gasped. "I feel as if I'm in some sort of dream. I only met you an hour or two ago and now

11

I'm letting you treat me like—like a call girl."

"Why not—a wife?" I whispered.

She shivered, still half in her dream world.

"I admit I haven't been myself lately," she murmured above my head. "Ever since I had that accident in Paris—ooooh, you must stop! I—I can't think straight when you're . . . doing that." Her soft palms cupped my face. Instead of lifting my mouth away from her, she moved my lips from one breast to the other.

"You do too much thinking," I breathed. "It's time you relaxed a little. Everybody needs relaxation, even famous lady diplomats."

Her voice was a throaty murmur. "If I didn't know better, I'd think you were trying to seduce me, Professor Damon."

, My hand was moving inside her brassiere, sliding fingers under her breast. I could hear her panting above me. She damn well liked what I was doing. She could talk all she wanted, but she needed this loveplay the way a sick child needs medicine.

I got the breast out, so that its weight was held by the downpulled brassiere cup. It quivered, big and white and swollen, and the dark brown nipple was an inch long. I kissed her nipple while I freed her other breast. She was sighing steadily and she turned her torso sideways until her unkissed nipple almost touched my mouth. I drew it in, welcoming it with a lashing tonguetip.

Rhea Carson moaned.

I was affected myself. Kissing her heavy breasts, having seen her handsome legs in stockings and without, my maleness was being geared for what the French call *fruit d'amour.*

"We must stop," she whispered.

"Give me a reason," I breathed onto her wet nipple.

"We've only just met."

I kissed her other breast. "I could know you for ten years and not be any more aroused by your womanhood than I am right now."

"Are you aroused?"

"Find out for yourself."

She put a hand toward my loins, but drew it back instantly. Her body grew stiff against me as she pushed

12

herself away. "I must be mad!" she cried. She did not cover her breasts. They quivered naked in front of me as she lifted her hand and patted her hair in the gesture of the eternal woman.

I saw that her eyes were fever-bright and that her coloring was heightened. Maybe she wanted to put up a front, perhaps she wanted to make sure I didn't think she was a pushover, but Rhea Carson desperately needed bedding by a virile male, even if she didn't know it.

Naturally I was not going to fling myself at her as might an overheated schoolboy. I am a mature man. I have made love to women as a vocation and as an avocation. This woman wanted a sampling of the Damon technique, but I wanted her to know and accept that fact, admit it honestly to herself.

So when she got to her feet and stood looking down at me, her breasts bare, I did absolutely nothing. We locked stares. She drew in a deep breath.

"At least I stopped your hysteria," I smiled.

She blinked in surprise, then in sudden anger. She would not come out and tell me she wanted a love-in. She had to play the great lady. Maybe she even wanted me to make the first move so she could reject me and build her ego. It was possible; I've known women like that. Now I'd hurt that ego by as good as telling her I didn't think she was attractive enough to bed down.

"Is that why you did it?" she whispered.

"At first—yes."

Her pride clung to the two words. "At first?"

I reached out and hooked her behind a knee, bringing her down onto my lap. Her soft thigh felt my excited manhood. She pressed it while she tried to fight my arms that closed around her.

"Of course, at first," I explained. "But when I saw how attractive you are, it became for real. You know?"

She knew all right. Her thigh was tight against me. Rhea Carson tried the haughty bit. "All right, but you'd better let me go. We can't do anything about it. We have to continue our walking tour of the university."

"I don't think we'd better. I might not be able to save you next time."

The fear glinted in her eyes. Unconsciously she softened

13

the muscular structure of her body so that she lay soft and warm against me. I took advantage of her changed mood to slide her skirt up to her loins. My hands went between her soft thighs and upward.

Rhea Carson moaned, quivering.

"Damn you," she whispered. "I should have known when I learned you headed that League for Sexual Dynamics that you'd make a play for me."

I came damn near belting her. Instead, I made her suffer. My fingers went to work under her girdle. When she gave soft little cries as she writhed and twisted—not to free herself from my caresses but to spread them over a particular area—I knew I had her.

"Want to go walking?"

"Yes—no! Oh, damn you! Damon, you—no!"

She turned in my arms, threw an arm about my neck and kissed me with widespread lips. She moaned and panted in my open mouth, quivering in reaction to my fondling fingers. Her bared legs were wide apart, she was an honestly hungry woman.

"What do you want to do?" I breathed against her tongue, then bit it before she could answer.

At last she managed to gulp, "Bed me, bed me! I've never felt like this, all crazy, all shaking."

The hysteria was gone for sure.

She was turning, putting her hands down low on me, gripping me, clambering onto my lap with her thighs open. I think she wanted me to take her right there on my divan. I am no man for hurry-up jobs; a woman is a fine wine to be sampled slowly and carefully, especially the first time.

Her breath was coming and going right in my face. I had to slow her down before she got things too far along the way. My zipper was undone, her soft hand was inside holding me, trying to free me for her pleasure.

My thumbs and forefingers caught her stiff nipples, pinched them hard. She gave a cry of pain. Her green eyes blazed down at me as she straddled my legs.

"What'd you do that for?" she snapped.

"Don't rush!" I snapped. "We have all day. I want to enjoy this. I want you to enjoy it just as much."

"But I need it. I need you!"

I kissed each of her breasts before I said, "You're going

14

to need me even more, honey. Now stand up."

She slid backwards to the floor. I bent and caught her skirt, unzipping it, pushing it down past her girdled hips and shapely thighs. As she stepped out of it, she was standing naked in a crumpled black girdle gathered about her hips that hid nothing of her dark femininity, while her breasts were staring at me above her downpulled brassiere cups.

"Undress me," I ordered.

She nodded, biting her lower lips, staring at my open fly. Her body was fleshy, but not fat. There were red girdle marks on her hips where the updrawn girdle bared them. As a practicing sexologist, I studied her body with more than the normal interest of a soon-to-be-lover.

Her breasts were hemispherical, as are the great majority of breasts in the English-speaking world. Not for her the conical, the bowl, the elongated mammary of the rest of the world. In hemispherical breasts, the height is equal to the radius of their circumference. All this did not detract from their attractiveness; I mention it because I mentally noted it, myself.

The area of the areolas is always more sensitive than the rest of the breast because the skin there is thinner, and affords a more direct route to the nerves which send pleasurable sensations through the female body. Her nipples were long when erect, an individual peculiarity not restricted to white women alone. The ridges of her areolas were of the prominent type known as tubercular.

While I studied her body, she was undoing my shirt buttons, tugging my Hathaway out of my slacks. Her fingers flew to my belt buckle, undid it, began shrusting slacks and shorts downward. Her eyes widened in surprise at sight of my male power.

"Oh! Oh, my goodness!"

I caught her girdle and did some pushing myself. She helped me with a couple of thumbs at the upper girdle. It dropped and lay on the carpet as I put my arms around her waist and lifted her, carrying her like that toward the bedroom.

She opened her thighs and caught hold of me, in a teasing grip, laughing softly, "My stallion!" She giggled, rubbing her thighs together.

"You've been around, I take it?"

She flushed, then laughed, turning to kiss my cheek. "I've been around. Yes, I'm not always the lady diplomat, sometimes I'm just a wanting woman. Like now."

I dropped her to her bare feet on the bedroom carpeting. She whirled and threw her arms about me, giving me the feel of her naked front. Her mouth was a moist invitation to venery, her tongue, as it flicked against mine, a silent voice that called to me imploringly.

I pushed her backward. Her legs hit the mattress edge, she fell onto the coverlets. Instantly I was with her, drawing her nude body to mine. My head bent, my lips went across her hardened breasts. As she moaned and ran her fingers through my hair, I kissed down her torso to her navel, and below.

Her hips turned and twisted. Her voice was a soft wail in the room. The hands that held my head were gentle, almost pleading, as they swung my face this way and that for her better enjoyment.

When neither she nor I could wait any longer, she drew me upward and between her quivering thighs. She gasped, she shook, her tongue licking the swollen wetness of her mouth, as I fed pleasure into her flesh.

My staying powers in the love embrace are extraordinary, my ability to prolong the sexual act a physical peculiarity.

I have enjoyed this phenomenon of a constantly erect penis a long time, ever since my boyhood and my first venture into the games of love. Some men might regard this priapic facility as a curse, because orgasm is often delayed for hours, if not entirely.

The orgasm pattern in the male consists of four parts. First, the excitement phase, during which his body is conditioned to the coming orgasm by kisses and caresses. Then occurs the plateau phase, during which the generative apparatus is functioning. There is erection, a change in breathing, an increase in blood pressure and pulse rate. Muscles strut and the spermatic cord shortens. In my own case, the plateau phase can continue indefinitely.

There is no third phase, as such, in priapism. The normal orgasm is the third phase, followed by the recovery.

But since my body never peaks in the love spasm, I am empowered to maintain phase three *ad infinitum*. This results in much delight for my love partner, whom I am able to carry over the brink of orgasmic pleasure again and again, without a halt.

A woman is constituted quite differently from a man in this regard. One or two orgasms, and the normal man is finished. The woman can go on in a steady stream of pleasure peaks so intense as to make her faint. There are attested cases in which women had a dozen or more orgasms, one after the other.

As Rhea Carson was doing right now.

She did not know about my priapism. All she knew was that I was damn near killing her with *zon-zon*. She wailed, head thrown backwards, she snarled with her teeth buried in my shoulder; she babbled out her delight and awe even as her buttock-play threatened to hurl us off the bed.

At ten minutes past one in the afternoon, Rhea Carson fainted. Her body went limp, her head rolled on the crumpled sheet where it rested. I let myself slide away from her, I lay back and stared at the ceiling.

I was worried about Rhea Carson. Our hours together in my bedroom had taught me that no matter what the rest of the world thought of my lady diplomat she was a woman who enjoyed life. Her aptitude to learn—as a test, I had swung her into the reverse supine posture, which they call *oolund-poolud* in India, then into the *purushayat*, where I lay on my back while she crouched over me—told me she was not suicide-prone. She loved performing *mukhmuttunih* on me, and having me please her with the French term *faire minette*. No manic-depressive can act *that* way!

Why then had she tried to kill herself?

There was no doubt of it being a suicide attempt. She had been standing beside me at the crosswalk as the car had approached. We had not been walking, just standing. And when the car neared, she had hurled herself in its path.

She stirred beside me. "Rod? What time is it?"

"Going on two. Come on, I'll take you out to lunch!"

"After I bathe?"

She turned over on her belly, smiling at me. I clapped

17

her soft buttock. "All right. Go take your bath. I'll wait, then take a fast shower."

She got off the bed and walked naked into the bathroom. She did not bother to close the door; after all we had done, neither of us held any secrets from the other. She bent over the tub, running water into it. She found some bubble bath crystals and scattered them about generously.

I stared at the ceiling and tried to think. I failed to notice her when she came back into the bedroom and began looking here and there in closets, even under the bed. At last she found what she wanted in the hall closet. An electric heater, fan-blown. She carried it into the bathroom and shut the door.

I reached for a cigarette.

"Holy good God!" I rasped, and leaped.

I ran for the bathroom door, I twisted the doorknob, I hurled myself in. If I was wrong, I was going to look like one damned fool.

I was not wrong.

She had plugged the heater into the shaving socket. It rested now on the floor beside the tub, its coils glowing cherry red. Sopping wet, Rhea was naked in the frothy water of the bath, half out of the tub as she reached for the electric heater.

If that heater went into the tub water, Rhea Carson would electrocute herself as surely as if she caught hold of a live wire. I leaped from the door toward the heater.

I could never bend and grab the damned thing. I had no time. She held it in her hands, raising it to drop it in the water. Her blank eyes saw me and did not know me.

My leg went out. I caught the heater with my bare foot and drove it through her hands toward the back of the tub. It hit the edge of the tub and slid down into the water.

But my kick had been so powerful that I'd unplugged the heater as I sent it flying. Rhea Carson was safe, and quite alive. Alive, yes; meaning, not dead. But there was no spirit, no soul, nothing behind her blank eyes.

I bent over the tub. I had no interest in her heavy breasts and their dark brown nipples, both of which were shiny with bath water, nor in her dimpled navel or her hips, or anything else. Only her eyes interested me.

18

They stared up at my face like those of a dead woman. I caught her wrists and shook her arms. She was like a newborn baby.

"Rhea! Rhea! Listen to me! Can you hear me?"

"I hear you. Yes, I hear you."

"Why did you do it? Why did you lift the heater to put it in the water?"

"I was cold. Cold! Freezing! The water was like ice."

I put my hand in the water and yanked it out damn fast. It was almost boiling, that bubble-bath frothiness.

"The water is hot, Rhea. Just think about it."

My hands held her wrists, my eyes searched her face. Slowly, very slowly, color came back into her cheeks. Her eyes darkened to sudden understanding.

"Rod—I did it again, didn't I?"

There was stark terror on her pretty face. She knew now all right. The knowledge was hitting her fast, and below the belt. She bent forward, moaning.

"Why, Rhea? Why?"

"I do-don't know. I don't!"

I got to my feet. I lifted the electric heater and carried it with me into the bedroom. At the door I said, "Wash yourself. I'm going to take steps this doesn't happen to you again. And leave the door open this time."

I didn't want her drowning herself.

I began dialing the telephone, but I kept staring into the bathroom to make sure my lady diplomat didn't try any more stunts. My ear waited for the telltale voice.

"Hello? Who's there?"

I knew that gruff voice better than I knew my own. It belonged to my Chief of Operations, the man who sent me out across the world whenever the Thaddeus X. Coxe Foundation decided a Coxeman was needed to keep the forces of law and order intact. Or when somebody high up wanted to do just the opposite.

Ever since Walrus-moustache had practically kidnapped me and talked me into taking part in what later became known as The Berlin Wall Affair, I have been leading a double life. I have become expert in judo, karate and savate. I have been a secret agent in almost any country you can name. I have killed, I have stolen, I have discovered I am a damn good shot with a rifle or a revol-

19

ver. In short, I am two men: a professor and a paid professional spy.

Every once in a while I start the action.

Like now.

I talked fast. Walrus-moustache can listen when he must, when he understands that things are serious. He asked a couple of pertinent questions, and I could almost see his shaggy-haired head nodding at my answers.

Then: "Hold the fort, Professor. I'm on my way. I may be delayed a bit because I want Doc Thayer to come along with me."

Doctor Clinton Thayer was a neurosurgeon, one of the most brilliant in the world. He was at the university to give a series of lectures during the next week. I don't know how Walrus-moustache expected to get him to drop everything and come along, but I'd long ago given up wondering how Old Handlebars did it.

I just sat there staring at Rhea Carson in the bathtub after I put down the phone. Until she got out of the tub, that is, and reached for a bath towel. Then I went into the bathroom and dried her down.

My voice clued her in on what I had done, while my hands went over her soft flesh with the Cannon. She was annoyed at first, but only on the surface. Deep down, she was damn happy the decision had been taken out of her hands.

"He'll think I'm crazy!" she wailed.

"Then a psychiatrist will cure you."

Her smile was rueful. "I suppose you're right. Though it isn't every day I face up to the problem of whether I'm going mad or not."

"Maybe you aren't going mad. Maybe there's another explanation," I commented.

"Like what?" she demanded.

That one, I couldn't answer.

I managed to get her into her brassiere, blouse and skirt before Old Handlebars rang my doorbell. We did not bother with the girdle and her stockings. I had the feeling Thayer would order her into the university hospital, and she wouldn't need underwear there.

I also fed her three martinis. I had two myself.

Walrus-moustache bulked big in the doorway, his face

serious, almost drawn. Just beyond him a stocky man with balding head and graying hair was fiddling with his tie. Doctor Clinton Thayer. At first glance, his face appeared to have an abstracted look, as though he dreamed on other worlds. Later I was to understand that his mind was always active, that he could think three different thoughts and speak a fourth all at the same time.

Rhea seemed shy as they came into the living room. Walrus-moustache bowed politely and introduced the doctor. Then he settled down in a big wing chair.

"You must think I'm a nut," Rhea said to the doctor. "I'd never have bothered you. Professor Damon was worried, though, and he did the phoning."

"May I touch your head, Mrs. Carson?" Thayer asked.

She looked the surprise I felt, but she nodded and half turned her pretty face away. The doctor put his hands on her head, feeling all over it. Twice he nodded, then a jerk of his head drew Walrus-moustache out of the chair.

"Put your hands where mine are," said Thayer.

Walrus-moustache did as told. After his fingers felt her skull for a few moments, he nodded, and his face was ashen. His hard glance raked me, and then the doctor.

"We'll need the utmost secrecy," he muttered.

"Naturally, naturally. I know Doctor Holmes of the Caldwell Neurosurgical Clinic." Thayer turned to me. "May I use your phone?"

Rhea swung about with half a laugh on her lips. "I do appreciate your secrecy, but it isn't necessary to——"

Walrus-moustache bowed. "Mrs. Carson, you are the victim of a plot that is aimed not only at compelling you to kill yourself, but possibly at control of the entire world."

I knew it was going to happen some day. Old Handlebars had finally done it. He had flipped his wig. Rhea cried out in rejection of his ominous words too.

"Have you been in the hospital—any hospital—during the past three months, Mrs. Carson?"

"Certainly not! I'm—or was—as healthy as a horse! I've had no need of medication for—ohhh!"

She sat there, staring blankly. After a moment she lifted her eyes to the chief. "How did you know?" she asked softly.

21

"It was Doctor Thayer who told me there might be a possibility of it, on our way over here. I was merely asking a question he is certain to ask you."

"But I was in that hospital for a touch of food poisoning. It happened in Paris! There's a small, private hospital just outside Dampierre, where an ambulance brought me. Food poisoning! Certainly that could never affect my head or my brain!"

"You were under sedatives for a while?"

"Yes. For about two days, I believe."

"It happened then."

I interrupted. "Don't be so mysterious. What happened then? And why should some two-bit hospital in Paris want to harm Rhea Carson?"

"Let me answer that," said Doctor Thayer, emerging from my bedroom where he had been phoning. "First of all, it isn't any two-bit hospital that treated her. Secondly, they want Rhea Carson dead because her diplomatic abilities might bring peace to Israeli and Arabs, and the men who own and operate that hospital don't want anything like that to happen. So—they tell Rhea Carson to kill herself."

I was gaping, my mouth open. I asked, "But how could anybody compel her to do that?"

"That," said Walrus-moustache, "is exactly what we are going to find out."

He gestured and Rhea Carson got to her feet.

Like a trained animal, like a robot.

CHAPTER TWO

She lay beneath a sheet in the Operation room of the Caldwell Neurosurgical Clinic under sedation. Her head was shaven clean. I had been watching behind a surgical mask, completely sterilized and in a baggy wraparound as, one by one, Doctor Clinton Thayer, under the keen eyes of Doctor Lawrence Holmes, had delicately removed three tiny stimulators from her scalp.

I saw the three little buttons, and shivered, as each was lifted out of place. They were more than buttons, of course; they were highly developed, miniaturized radio receivers capable of receiving radio impulses from long distances. Just as electrodes could receive and act upon electricity, so these stimulators could act upon radio signals.

Doctor Thayer nodded, his eyes dark and brilliant above his surgeon mask. "Take over, nurse," he murmured, and began stripping off his gloves. At the same moment he gestured at Walrus-moustache and me where we were elbow to elbow near the far wall of the room, just to one side of the oxygenator machine.

As we went out into the hall, Doctor Thayer said, "It's what I expected. You saw for yourselves. There were three stimulators. Each one affected a different section of the brain. The thalamus, which serves the brain as a memory bank; the hypothalamus, which controls the breathing, heartbeat, thirst, appetite; and the amygdala, which may be said to be concerned with suicidal tendencies, since it regulates the emotional factors of the human body."

I took out a pack of cigarettes, passed it around, and lighted everybody up. Then I asked, "Do you mean to tell

23

me that a man could have sent out a radio signal that would make Rhea kill herself?"

"Of course, Professor Damon. That's what this is all about." Doctor Thayer smiled grimly. "It has scary implications, doesn't it? There's a theory that President Kennedy was assassinated by a man under such control, you know."

Walrus-moustache grunted. "Let's give him the course."

We followed the medico into a big electronics laboratory, filled with banks of controls all along the walls. Counters were thick with toys and gadgets. I watched as Thayer lifted off one such gadget and put it on the floor. He turned to one of the electronic switchboards and began throwing a couple of the switches.

The gadget he had put on the floor was a kind of six wheeled vacuum cleaner. It began buzzing, moving as it buzzed. A dirt bag that had been folded flat on its metal back filled with air and stood straight up. The bug-cleaner ran all around, sucking in dirt.

"A simple mechanism, designed to function on a single motive-track," Thayer murmured. "A machine, controlled by an electronic brain built inside it. Nothing more. A scientist named Berkeley has built a number of such gadgets, including a tick-tack-toe machine that cannot be beaten, as well as a number of other fascinating gadgets.

"But this is only the beginning. Operational control of a mechanical brain. The frightening thing is, what can be done to a mechanical brain can also be done to a human brain, since the mechanical brain is always patterned after the human one."

I murmured, "In other words, Rhea Carson was something like that electronic vacumm cleaner, only on a higher scale."

Thayer nodded grimly. "She was conditioned to self-destruct, Professor."

His hand waved us forward to another section of the laboratory. There were two flat tables set almost side by side. Behind them were a number of metal boxes piled one upon the other, each with a series of dials and switches.

"We can test compatability between a man and a woman with these, or between two men who might be picked to spend months on the moon in the space program. The wave analyzer picks out the alpha patterns and matches them up. All brains give off electrical impulses. The analyzer studies them.

"The wave analyzer is sometimes called a 'love machine,' since the man and woman whose alpha patterns match exactly—as so many of them do—are said to be psychologically capable of falling in love with each other.

"As with people, so with animals. Come."

We left that laboratory and and went downstairs to another room, filled with cats, mice, monkeys, rats and such creatures. From one cage Thayer lifted a cat; from the other, a mouse. He set them in a single large cage.

Instantly the cat leaped for the mouse, pinning it under a paw. But Thayer was at a control bank, working the electronic impulses which would affect the behavior of both animals. Suddenly the cat leaped back, its back arched, its tail bushy. It was obviously terrified.

The mouse chased the cat—I got the feeling the mouse thought the cat was a chunk of cheese with legs—and the cat fled as if the mouse were the devil himself.

"Impossible behavior, you may say," said Thayer, shutting off his machine and putting the animals back in their cages. "No cat in the world is afraid of a mouse. This cat was, because the normal functions of its brain have been interfered with. Electronic impulses make it afraid. Electronic impulses make the mouse fierce."

"I'm getting the picture," I announced.

The doctor smiled. "It isn't a picture we can take with any sang-froid. We can look ahead, being reasoning men, to a situation such as that in which Rhea Carson found herself. She was never herself since she left Paris. She was nothing more than a robot, existing only at the will of the men who put those receivers in her head."

"Is she safe now?"

"Oh, yes. There aren't any more receiving sets in her to trigger off her emotions. We took them all out."

Old Walrus-moustache spoke for the first time from the shadows where he bulked large. "How is this accomplished, Doctor? What do those impulses do in the human brain?"

Thayer crushed out his cigarette. "Well, we know first

of all, that the human brain is the seat for all human behavior. The brain sends out the commands that move the body, sometimes in reaction to a message it has received from—say, a hand too near a fire. Nerve relays send the heat message to the brain, the brain sends back the command to yank the hand away. All done in a fraction of a second. The force activating this system of nerve relays, brain and body, is electricity.

"Electroshock therapy can help cure certain mental disorders. Physicians can now locate brain tumors that cause certain types of human behavior, by the use of the electroencephalograph. Today we have what we doctors call ESB—electrical stimulation of the brain. You've seen it demonstrated in animals with the cat and the mouse. We've shied away from using it with human beings.

"Others are not so reluctant, as witness Rhea Carson."

A thought touched my mind. "You can cause an animal to hate and attack another. You could make the animal equally love the other animal, couldn't you?"

"Yes, indeed. No trouble at all. The amygdala is the seat of love and hate in the brain. It is that area of the brain located between the spetal region and the thalamus. Its role in human behavior is very sexual, Professor. If it is destroyed in a woman, she becomes a nymphomaniac. In a man, he becomes subject to satyrism.

"An electrical stimulation of the feline amygdala can make a cat grow affectionate, or savage. It can do the same thing in a woman, or a man. The pleasure centers of the brain can be electrically stimulated until a rat, for instance, will live only for that utter delight."

"Fascinating," I murmured. "Why, one of those buttons in the right brain might do away with marriage counselors."

The doctor was serious about it. "In time, we may come to that, Professor. In your studies as head of the Leauge for Sexual Dynamics, you might well consider the future of our 'love machine,' or even electronic controls of the human libido."

"I shall, indeed," I murmured.

"What about the receivers you removed from Rhea Carson?" asked Walrus-moustache.

"They are transistor-timed stimulators. With the advent

of the tiny transistor, there was no need to plug in wires to feed electricity to the brain. It can be done now on a timing basis or by broadcast of radio signals. An animal can be made to do almost anything by the proper stimulation of its motor cortex. Stop eating. Freeze into position without moving. You name it, the animal will do it. Like a robot responding to an electronic command."

Sweat broke out on my forehead. "Can you imagine an army of men with those buttons inside their skulls? They wouldn't feel pain. They would go on battling until they couldn't move. Then they would destroy themselves."

"This is what we're up against, Professor," murmured Thayer, with a wave of the hand. "Oh, we've known—or suspected—that certain forces in the world have been performing what we consider illicit operations upon human beings. If you want to dispose of someone, you plant a stimulator-receiver in his or her head. You don't have to hire an assassin. Your victim will conveniently commit suicide for you."

I shivered. "They wanted Rhea to kill herself so she wouldn't bollix up plans the opposition has for a renewed war in the Middle East between Israel and the Arab countries. And maybe even World War three. Alive, she might talk both sides into a peaceful settlement of the issues."

"Right on target," growled Walrus-moustache, moving out of the shadows where he had hidden himself. "And now to zero in on the bull's-eye. Damon, you're going to Paris."

"Whaaat?" I howled.

"You must recognize the necessity of flushing these birds from covert. We can't have them controlling the lives of people like Rhea Carson. Or anybody else, for that matter. You go to Paris, you let them operate on you——"

"Not on your moustache wax!"

Doctor Thayer grinned, "We would take precautions, Professor."

"What precautions?"

"We would plant an electronic pulsator in your body. It would break up the radio signals which would otherwise control you. You would feel an urge to do what the stimulator willed you to do—but you could overcome that urge by sheer will power."

"That's only theory," I pointed out.

"It was only theory that led to all the great discoveries in the world. Columbus had a theory. So did Edison, Marconi, Newton."

"Yeah. Well . . ."

Walrus-moustache chuckled. "It won't interfere with your love life, you know. It will be there to protect you from blind obedience to the opposition. No more, no less."

"You make it sound like I'm just going to take a birth control pill," I growled. I fidgeted, feeling helpless. I knew damn well I was going to agree to their plan for me. It was only a matter of time.

I threw up my hands. "Why argue? I never got anywhere arguing with you, anyhow. What do I have to do?"

Doctor Thayer became all business. "I will simply make a small incision somewhere in your body—I won't tell you where for fear you might inadvertently betray its whereabouts—and implant a time-transistor that will enable you to fight off the otherwise compulsive effects of any stimulator they put in your head."

"You're sure it'll work?"

"I guarantee it, Professor Damon."

"Okay, okay. Let's go get it over with."

I undressed in a little cubicle in the ward section of the Clinic. When I was naked, I rang a bell and a nurse brought in the wraparound I was to wear while on the table.

Her penciled eyebrows rose admiringly at sight of the Damon physique. I am proud of my body. I keep it in perfect muscular trim with judo, karate, savate exercises, as well as swimming, weight lifting and rowing. I have to be a perfect male specimen to stay alive when Walrus-moustache sends me off on those Coxeman activities he dreams up for me. I am six feet tall and I weigh a hundred and eighty pounds of solid muscle.

"Well, *hello* here," the redhead caroled.

I grinned. "I hope you're around when I come out of the ether. We could have things to talk about."

"I'll make it my business," she laughed, eyeing my loins.

"Come back when I come out of the ether, and we'll talk about it. I'll want to make sure they haven't made a eunuch out of me."

Her glowing brown eyes told me they had better not.

Walrus-moustache was with the orderly who wheeled the transfer table into my room. His thumb dismissed the nurse.

"Just stay easy, Damon," he growled at me. "This won't hurt you at all. In a day or two, you'll be up and about without any ill effects."

"Yeah, hey," I muttered, getting on the table.

The orderly wheeled me down the hall and into an elevator. The elevator delivered me to the operating room floor. The orderly delivered me to the operating table itself. Doctor Thayer was there behind his mask, slipping his hands into rubber gloves held by a pert nurse. I relaxed my muscles. For better or worse, I was committed. There was no getting out of it now, especially since the anesthetist was fitting a cup down over my nose and mouth.

I woke up in a dark room. I was very sleepy. I felt no pain, nothing but that desire to sleep. So I slept, just by closing my eyelids.

Three more times I came back to consciousness in an empty room. Each time I was sleepy as all hell. I have a vague recollection of somebody sticking a needle into my arm on one of these occasions. It made no nevermind to me.

The next time I opened the Damon eyelids, my redheaded nurse was standing beside the bed. So was Walrus-moustache.

"He's ready to leave, sir," Redhead murmured.

"Good. It's about time. You've been lying there four days, Damon. Under sedation. You won't be able to feel where Doctor Thayer inserted the transistor."

I wriggled around under the covers. He was right. I didn't feel the slightest twinge. So I glared at old Walrus-moustache. "If I'm going to get dressed, you might as well leave, Chief."

His chuckle was very understanding. Too much so. "Indeed I shall, but I'm going to take Miss Noren with me. We don't want you wasting your strength, now do we?"

The redhead pouted, but she went out into the hall.

I got ,dressed, cursing Walrus-moustache under my breath. He could have spared me a couple of hours to test my motor responses. I could have recouped my strength on my flight plane to Paris.

I must say the Coxe Foundation does things up brown. My luggage was packed, there was a ticket for Flight 23 on an Air France jet to Paris laid on top of the attache case which held my passport and a deadly, blued-steel Luger automatic with a leather holster harness that would fit under my left armpit.

I was set to trot.

A limousine took me to the airport after an hour-long briefing mission with Walrus-moustache in his traveling van. My job was simple. I was to be the guinea pig to be picked up and operated on by the opposition. While that was happening, I was to study the layout, make plans for its destruction and the capture of the opposition personnel.

The opposition was called HECATE, as near as the chief could judge. Rumors and bits of gossip had been gathered up by our boys in Paris and elsewhere, then sent home for appraisal. The pattern was beginning to emerge. HECATE was an organization dedicated to the proposition that anything justified the making of money. It was ready to operate on a man or a woman and get him or her to do anything from betray a trust to overthrowing a government, or even to killing herself.

It charged enormous fees, but its work was worth every penny, franc or shilling of them. In these days when so much power is concentrated in one or two men in various governments, it would be relatively simple, were an organization to take over those one or two men, to take over the governments themselves.

Paying a fee to HECATE was a hell of a lot cheaper than paying for a war, or even a revolution. One way or another, a HECATE agent could cause an accident—as witness Rhea Carson—then cause that accident victim to become whatever HECATE and the people paying the fee wanted him or her to become. Look around the world, decide how fast governments have been rising and falling. Greece. Indonesia. And others. Four or five men in high places can make a lot of trouble.

Walrus-moustache, from his analysis of the information he had at his fingertips, suspected a segment of the French people as being the brains behind HECATE. Maybe they had used Communist money to get started, but now they were pretty much self-sustaining. Maybe they were entirely independent of Communism. Nobody knew for sure. It was my job to find out.

Official France had no hand in HECATE. The chief was pretty damn certain about this. It was an independent crowd of Frenchmen, out to make money and usurp power, to make American and British diplomats look like bumbling idiots, to throw monkey wrenches into our statesmanship plans, to control by radio transmission the acts of individuals in high places so as to achieve the ends they had in mind.

HECATE would have kept an eye on Rhea Carson to make sure she killed herself. They would also know Professor Rod Damon had saved her life. Walrus-moustache had given the story of my rescue to the newspapers. HECATE would be out gunning for me, by this time. Walrus-moustache said he didn't think they wanted to kill me. The paper had given a list of my exploits as head of the L.S.D. HECATE would want to take control of my talents to do its dirty work, he was sure.

I hoped he was right.

If they wanted me dead, I was a sitting duck.

The French police would assist me, if necessary. So would the Coxe Foundation in Paris. I had a counter-transistor in me to negate the effects of the stimulator that would be put inside my head. Everything was coming up roses, according to plan. The way Walrus-moustache looked at it, I was on a vacation.

The Air France jet took off on time.

We were half an hour over the ocean when a stewardess in her baby blue uniform and pert cap brought me a martini. I sipped it, relaxing while I considered ways and means. Obviously, since I couldn't be sure the opposition had its eye on me, I must make certain I attracted their attention.

So when the stewardess came for my empty glass, I struck up a conversation. I told her I was on a holiday, that I was out for kicks, that money was no object. Could she tell me where I could find fun and games in gay Paree?

She could not, that was not part of her job. Her eyes twinkled as she told me this, she was *très sympathetique,* she would have liked to help but airline policy forbade.

"I respect that policy," I told her. "But you aren't working all the time. You must get some time off—like, after you report in when the flight is over. You're on your own then."

"I shall see, m'sieu," was all I could get out of her. As I watched her bottom wriggle off down the aisle under her tight baby blue skirt, I told myself I damn well would get more out of this little French chick.

Rhea had told me she had been taken sick at the Ane d'Or restaurant. Apparently, then, the opposition had agents planted in the Golden Ass eaterie. The Ane d'Or would be my first port of call when I went clattering about the Paris night spots.

I figured the stewardess would be a good cover for my activities, if I could inveigle her into going out on the town with me. I set myself to win her over. When I slipped a tip under my dishes at dinnertime, I made sure it was a ten-dollar bill.

Her thin black brows rose at sight of the sawbuck. She made a motion to hand it back to me, but suddenly her green eyes laughed and she tucked it up under her sleeve, bending forward to hide her action from curious eyes.

"You are a very silly man," she whispered. "I do not accept bribes."

"Ah, you must be married," I said confidently. "Your husband would beat you if he caught you with money of your own."

I had seen no wedding ring, no engagement ring. She flushed faintly and tossed her head. "I am not married. Nor engaged. I am my own woman."

An independent sort. There would be no entanglements, then. I said casually, "I'm going to hire a car when I get to Paris. I have a couple of weeks free time and I want to spend it doing fun things. I really do need a companion. You see, I suffer from monophobia."

She whisked off down the aisle, buttocks jerking, a puzzled look on her face. I could see her whispering to the other stewardesses, and they all kept glancing at me from time to time. At least I had attracted attention on the plane. Now if I could do the same thing in Paris. . . .

"Would you like a pill, m'sieu?" asked my stewardess.

"A pill? Why should I want a pill?"

"If you are ill, you take a pill."

I smiled. "Monophobia doesn't mean I'm sick. It means I'm afraid of—a certain thing."

"And what is that?"

"I'll tell you tonight, if you'll go out with me."

Her green eyes were puzzled. She stared down at me, drew a deep breath—I got the impression of upstanding breasts under her white blouse—and sighed. She shook her head, on which the Air France cap was perched, and shrugged her shoulders with Gallic fatalism.

"I think you are a very naughty man, m'sieu," she announced finally. "And you have an approach that is very unique."

"I'm a very shy man."

"Ha! You are a *papillon*."

A libertine? Well, maybe. I just winked at her.

I noticed that all the other stewardesses eyed me slyly as they went back and forth. I began to feel like Bluebeard. I also noticed that a small, dapper man in a pin-stripe suit was looking at me from time to time with something like cold speculation in his eyes. I felt like a turkey being assayed for the chopping block. Maybe I was getting the attention I wanted.

The rest of the flight was uneventful.

Over Orly Airport, my stewardess bent to whisper, "I'll meet you in the waiting room, m'sieu—after you have collected your luggage. I want to return your ten-dollar bill."

She was sitting on a lounge chair with her legs crossed. She had good legs. I would have noticed her even if I didn't have a date to meet her. She smiled as I made a little bow.

"I have a taxi waiting, mam'selle," I announced. "It will deliver me to the Plaza-Athénée hotel. But before it does, it will permit me to see you to your home."

She nodded and fell into step beside me.

Yvette Crillaire lived in a small apartment house on the Left Bank, not far from the Jardin des Plantes. She was very determined I should not see her to her rooms, pleading the fact that she needed a long hot bath and a nap. So I settled for a date at eight that night, during which she would show me the parts of Paris a tourist rarely sees.

She hesitated, then asked, "This monophobia. What is it?"

"A mortal fear of being alone," I smiled. "That's why I need a companion. Oh, by the way, a friend of mine told me about the Ane d'Or. Is it the 'in' thing to go there? I was advised not to miss it."

"We shall see it, yes. And one or two other places." Her green eyes were overbright. "I think you are the libertine, m'sieu. So I am going to assume you might like the naughty show, hein? The one held in a cellar club?"

"You assume right, honey," I nodded, figuring that HECATE would prefer to get in its dirty work in dimly lighted, out-of-the-way bistros rather than in a place like the Folies Bergère.

I patted her behind as she stepped past me to the sidewalk. Her giggle sounded as promising as her soft buttocks felt. Her gloved fingertips waved me a farewell as the taxi rocketed away from the curb.

The Plaza-Athénée is one of the better hotels in Paris, though not in the class of the Ritz or the Crillon. Since I do not like to wear a tie at all times, and since the Ritz, for one, insists on this bit of frou-frou, I had selected the hotel on the Avenue Montaigne.

However, I did splurge a bit in the selection of my rooms. They were located on the top floor, one of those new and yacht-like suites with low ceilings and a price tag of over seventy dollars a day. It was Coxe Foundation money, so I treated myself right. Besides, the restaurant here is one of the finest hotel eateries in all Paris.

Like the girl I was dating that night, I took a hot bath and slept until after five in the afternoon. The time difference between Europe and the States always leaves me

34

woozy. I shook that wooziness between the sheets.

At eight sharp I was on the Rue Larrey, stepping out of the taxi to pick up Yvette Crillaire. I had a bottle of Lentheric perfume in one hand and two dozen long-stemmed roses in the other. I was determined to overwhelm my pretty stewardess with attention.

Unfortunately it was not Yvette who opened her apartment door, but her roommate, a girl with long tawny hair and blue eyes. She had a mini-skirted cocktail dress out of which her bare shoulders and upper breasts rose in a cloud of perfume.

"I'm so sorry," she apologized, stepping back so I could enter the tastefully furnished rooms, "but Yvette was summoned away by a long-distance phone call to visit her sick mother."

It was a horrendous excuse, but I bore up under it, confident that the blonde was here to substitute for her. I remembered the dapper man in the pin-stripe suit on the plane, and now I felt certain he was from HECATE. So too was—

"My name is Claudette Marly," she smiled.

I made her a little bow and extended the perfume and the roses. Her look of surprise was enchanting. At least HECATE had done me the honor of baiting the hook with a real goody.

"*Pour moi?*" she breathed.

"In the absence of Yvette, and in the hope that you'll consent to take her place. She was going to show me the naughtier side of Paris."

"Oh, I could do that," she told me, blue eyes flirting at me over the two dozen roses. "I know very many bistros where the floor shows are quite exciting. You would wish one of those, hein?"

"I would indeed," I admitted.

Her soft laughter told me she saw the way I was staring at her mounded breastflesh quivering naked above her low bodice. She shook her shoulders, making those *coussins* jiggle loosely. Her eyes flirted with mine when I took the time to look into their blue depths.

She handed me her black velvet evening wrap to hold while she settled her smooth shoulders in it. Then her arm hooked mine and we were on our way.

35

We dined at the Tour d'Argent on pressed duck, wine and champagne. This restaurant is perhaps the oldest eaterie in Paris, and its dining rooms overlook the Seine River and Notre Dame cathedral. It is a fabulous sight by night. When I could take my eyes off my companion and those breasts that threatened to pop into sight at any moment, I admired the view beyond the window.

A four-thousand-franc gratuity to the maître d' had assured us of a most excellent table under the maroon and white drapes, where one could stare at the lights of Paris. I watched respect creep into the eyes of Claudette Marly as I made certain this was going to be a night to be remembered.

The condemned man ate a hearty meal, I was thinking as I savored the duck. We who are about to die, salute you. And all that jazz.

For I was convinced little Claudette was from HECATE, and that before the evening was over, HECATE would strike at me.

Until that moment, however, I was determined to have a good time. So after the tartes aux fraises for dessert, and excellent coffee, I guided my blonde beauty toward a taxi stand. I explained that the rest of the evening was at her discretion, and for her not to be too discreet.

"We shall go to Les Choses d'Amour," she announced firmly.

"The arts of love," I translated. "It sounds promising."

She giggled, "Oh, it isn't known by that name alone. Just as l'Entrecote disguises itself behind the name of Relais de Venise, and the Chope d'Orsay under the title, Enjalbert, so the Love Arts is also called the Way of Life. There is a cellar attached to the upstairs restaurant. It is to the cellar we will go."

To the cellar we went, down a flight of narrow stairs in which the wooden treads were hollowed out by countless feet bound on the same sort of errand we were on this night. I got the feeling that Claudette Marly wanted to have herself a good time before turning me over to her bosses.

The cellar was surprisingly clean, with tiny tables set with checkered tablecloths and lone candles. The candles gave off the only light in the bistro except for the

36

spotlights on the small stage, that served also as a dance floor. Intimacy was the order of the day for Les Choses d'Amour.

There was a show going on as we slipped between the tables. Two naked girls were in the last stages of a lesbian love-in, writhing and twisting about in the traditional *soixante-neuf* position. I stared at jellying buttocks and jiggling breasts while I fumbled for a chair.

A pretty girl in an apron and high heels clicked those heels in our direction as she hurried toward us. There was nothing above or below the apron except bare girl.

Claudette giggled, "She is pretty, yes?"

I patted her bottom. "Almost as pretty as you, cherie."

"Two absinthes," Claudette murmured.

I blinked. Absinthe is a verboten drink in the States. To much of an aphrodisiac, or so they say. It has a sweet licorice taste, but it really hits you below the belt. Or where you live.

"On the rocks," I amended, hoping the ice would slow down the action. I didn't want to lose my inhibitions too quickly.

The girls on the couch in the spotlight were jerking furiously, heads caught between soft white thighs that rippled in orgasmic fury. I felt my mouth go dry. I needed no absinthe—the French call it Herbsaintes—to get me in the mood. There is a little of the voyeur in my makeup. I am geared to react to visual stimulation.

But when the greenish liqueur was set before me, I sipped it. By this time the lesbians had run offstage and a girl with a French poodle attached to a strap sauntered out in their place.

The girl was a redhead with very white skin and was quite pretty. Her costume consisted of shoes and stockings with a black garterbelt, with cuffs about her wrists, a collar of white pique at her neck, and a pert hat on her neatly coiffed red hair. Otherwise, she was stark naked. I gathered the cuffs and collar were to suggest she was fully dressed for boulevard strolling.

The dog was excited. I realised it had been fed some drug, maybe even a bowl of absinthe. It kept sniffing at the stockinged legs of its mistress and trying to stand on

37

its hind legs. Suddenly, I became aware of a second girl pacing forward out of the candlelit shadows.

She was also a redhead and wore exactly the same garments as her twin. The only difference was that instead of a dog at the end of her leather leash there was a naked young man.

As the dog acted, so did the man. He sniffed, he reared up, his tongue licked a soft thigh above the stockingtop. The redhead pushed him away as the other girl pushed the poodle. It was a well-rehearsed pantomime. It offered you a bit of bestiality along with the *besogne*.

The man was on his knees, the dog was on its hindlegs. Each was engaging in a bit of tongue-play on the two redheads. The women stood with heads thrown back, their hips jerking to involuntary spasms.

You could hear the redheads breathing harshly, a panting that was echoed by damn near everybody in the cellar cafe. I know my breath was harsh, and Claudette was going like a bellows as she stared.

I put a hand on her chair and slid it a few inches toward me. She did not take her eyes from the redheads, but her lips quirked in a tiny smile. The smile widened as my hand fell on her stockinged knee and slipped upward along her inner thigh.

I had no qualms about such conduct in public, not in a bistro like Les Choses d'Amour. It was what you paid your francs for, this intimate informality. Out of the corner of my eye I could see other men fondling their girlfriends. One woman had her thighs spread so wide I could see up under her skirt and observe the fact that she wore no undergarments.

My own hand was discovering the same thing about Claudette Marly. She was tightening her thighs on my hand, then loosening them in a steady rhythm which set up pulsations deep within her flesh. The feel of moist flesh plus the sight of the man and the animal in the dog collars and what they were doing to the redheaded girls was enough to make the absinthe bubble in my veins.

The redheads were sitting on chairs on either side of a table that had somehow replaced the couch where the lesbians had been performing. The women had their legs up on the table, crossed at their ankles. The audience had a good view of their snowy thighs and the *lampes amoureuses* between them.

The man and the dog were very busy with those exposed parts. The women were trying to control their emotions, but those loving tongues were very expert. One girl was biting her lower lip hard, eyes wide.

Claudette moaned, turning to catch my lips with hers, a hand at the back of my neck. Her hips jerked wildly against my hand for long moments. At the same time, her hand fell on my *penart* with a gentle grip.

"Mon Dieu," she breathed, *"tu etes envitaille!"*

"Thanks, honey. Not only am I well hung, I'm something of a perpetual motion machine as well. You want to find out?"

Her lips were quivering uncontrollably; at the moment she was beyond speech. I needed no other invitation. I swung her up onto my lap, raising her skirt to her pelvic bones. Her back was to me, in the seated *Venus reversa* position.

She took me easily, hips grinding downward until I was a part of her. Then she commenced a gentle rotation that was pleasing but not exhausting. I stared over her bare shoulder at the show.

The redheads were on their hands and knees on the long table, facing one another. The poodle was on its hind legs, the man was kneeling. All four performers were in violent motion.

A woman was wailing somewhere. A man was shouting hoarsely. I could hear Claudette Marly making little sounds as she increased her own tempo. Between those throaty cries, I heard her apologizing.

"I wanted to—make it last longer—but I cannot control myself," she was sobbing. "I must—must—"

The kneeling redheads and Claudette screamed at exactly the same moment. My arms were about the blonde French girl, holding her tightly, well aware that the *casse-noisette* action of her vaginal muscles was trying to coax me into the orgasmic spasm.

Claudette Marly did not know I was afflicted with that sex peculiarity which permits a man to maintain his rigidity endlessly during the sexual congress. It is an ailment—if so I can term it—which stands me in good stead

39

as the founder and number one instructor for my League of Sexual Dynamics. It also helps more than somewhat when I am on a Coxe Foundation job.

Like now, man. My pussycat partner was going off all over the place, bouncing and flopping, yelping her fleshly delight as I went right on staying with her. We were starting to attract attention, for one of the redheads was turning and staring at us, a friendly grin on her lips.

I heard a woman pant, "Will you look at them? He's been that way for ages. Sure I peeked. Hell, who wouldn't, with his equipment?"

And Claudette sobbed, *"Cracher! Cracher! Mon Dieu—cracher!"*

"I can't, honey," I breathed. "It's a kind of problem of mine. I stay like this indefinitely."

"You do?" Her surprise was laughable, except for the grotesque contortion of her lust-maddened face. "Honestly? You aren't ki-kidding me?"

"Try me," I invited.

She pulled free and slipped back into her chair. Her glance around the candlelit room was almost embarrassed. "Let's get out of here. We can go to my room. But please—hurry."

I gathered that HECATE was almost ready to pounce, and that my little honey-pot wanted more of the goodies before the trap snapped shut. Well, this was fine with me. I can never get too much of a good thing.

The price of two absinthes at Les Choses d'Amour is thirty thousand francs. Almost fifty bucks American. But hell, you got a floor show, and I was charging it up to the Coxe Foundation. As I made myself presentable, I figured I could do a paper on the act the two redheads put on, and file it under international relations in League headquarters.

We emerged into the night air, Claudette clinging amorously to me, rubbing her mound against my thigh. She was as heated-up as a female mink in season, and I congratulated myself on my cleverness in choosing as a date an Air France stewardess who had such a roommate.

In the taxi, she searched for my mouth blindly, eyes closed and lips open. She was all for mounting me, kneeling on the seat on either side of my thighs, but I tried to convey the idea I was too modest for that sort of thing. I mean, we were driving down the Boulevard Saint Germain, and even if it was the Latin Quarter, I had some shreds of decency left.

So I treated her to the *eplucher des lentilles,* which is finger-play of the female body, for close to twenty minutes. She was actually crying real tears, so emotionally explosive had she become.

I had to help her out of the taxi, and half support her with an arm about her middle as I led her into her apartment house. Her shapely gams were like rubber. In the tiny elevator, she clung to me as if afraid I would turn into mist.

I put her key in the lock, turning the doorknob.

Her hand flicked on the light switch. Two men were sitting there in easy chairs, hardbitten characters who stared at me with cold fish eyes. Claudette Marly gaped at them in dumb surprise.

The anger flushed her red. "Stupid pigs!" she screeched. "You're too early! Goddammit, you weren't supposed to come here until dawn!"

I guess she figured she had said enough to make me more than suspicious, because she turned her wide, tearful eyes in my direction and waved her hands in Gallic frustration.

"I am sorry, Professor," she cried. "I'd hoped to enjoy your ailment for another few hours—but these *bougres* care nothing for human relationships. They are too busy with their business."

"And what is their business?" I asked politely.

Nobody said a word. The men got out of the easy chairs and each one hunched his shoulders and wriggled his fingers a little, as a man does when he is about to engage in a simple form of exercise. I gathered these pigs were about to take a spot of boxing exercise, with me as the punching bag. Oddly enough, I liked the idea.

It is not a nice feeling to come home to her apartment with a chick like Claudette Marly and find a couple of strongmen there to prevent you from the bed-bouncing you had in mind. I was mad as hell, to be quite frank about it. Sure, before this was over I was going to be subdued and lugged off to that hospital in Dampierre, but

41

there was nobody to say I shouldn't have myself some satisfaction from them first.

They came toward me, walking on their toes. I guess that was to impress me as to how catlike and agile they were. Well, I was one mouse who was going to fight back.

I let them get three feet away.

Then I dropped flat and lashed out with a foot at the leg nearest me. My shoe landed with a solid thunk. From floor level I looked up grinning as the thug I'd just kicked opened his mouth, rolled his eyes and hopped up and down on one leg.

I swiveled around on my knees and belted his good leg with my shoulder, sending him flying backward across a tea table. Wood splintered. The lamp on the table went hurtling through the air to land in a crescendo of shattered porcelain and broken lamp bulb. The big bruiser bounced around in the midst of all this, bellowing out his aches and pains.

The other man dived at me.

He left his feet, both hands outstretched to grab my neck and choke me into submission. His face was pockmarked, his eyes were narrow slits between puffy eyelids, his clothes were a shade above the average. The thought touched my mind as I scrambled out of his way, that he was the main man in this duo. He would be the boss, the giver of the orders.

I did not scramble fast enough. His two hundred pounds and more came down across my thighs, damn near breaking them. A stab of pain shot along my nerve-ends just as he got a hand ready to slam me in an extremely delicate spot. There was a no-nonsense air about this boy, he was here to get a job done and he intended to get it over with as soon as possible.

I twisted my hips, took his blow on my hip-bone.

"*Non, non! Merde!* You will ruin him as a man!" Claudette screeched.

A lot he cared, the big *merde!*

Sitting there with him across my legs, I slammed the edge of a hand across his already-broken nose. He howled his anguish, getting to his knees and covering his nose with his big hands. I let my foot fall into his belly, with all my weight behind it.

42

He oofed and doubled up, retching.

I whirled, hunting the other bruiser but not seeing him in time as he shot forward across the broken table, the top of his head aimed at my face like he was a goat. His skull crunched into my cheek. I saw stars.

I twisted sideways, commanding my brain to forget the pain. My brain disobeyed me, because I felt it for sure. It made me even madder.

My fist let go with a wallop.

My knuckles hit a jawbone. If I hadn't been sitting on the floor when I let that blow go, so that it had little steam behind it, I would have knocked him out. As it was, he rolled aside, shouting curses.

Hey, I told myself. Don't win this fight!

Old Walrus-moustache expected me to get taken into that hospital and have my head operated on, to have a radio-thought-control stimulator placed in the fleshy part of my skull. I wouldn't be playing fair with the Thaddeus X. Coxe Foundation if I knocked these strongmen out.

So I had to ease up on the rough stuff. This wasn't as easy as it sounds. I had to make it look good, because Claudette Marly was there cheering me on, waving her pretty little fists around in the air, urging me to bop them some more.

I thrrew a wild right at the guy with the splinters from the shattered tea table sticking into him. It was deliberately off target. I wanted him to think I was close to the end of my roughhouse rope.

I guess I overacted. With a roar of happiness he ducked my fist and slammed me one in the ear. My head rang like it was a bell and it was Bastille Day in Paris.

The guy with the pockmarked face was himself again and joined in the attack on me from the rear. His hand-edge hit my throat a glancing blow. I sagged, waiting.

They took the bait. They leaped for me from opposite directions. I reached out, grabbed a tie and a shirt-front and tried to bang their heads together. I was partially successful at that.

Pockmark hit the splintery bruiser on his Adam's apple. The man with the splinters gagged and choked. My hands caught the tie I held, tightened it with a somewhat vicious tug.

43

The pockmarked face got purple.

Claudette screeched, "Oooooh—what a man! He can fight and *flon-flon* like a Hercules!"

Well, now. I might not go that far in praising myself, but I was more than holding my own. However, all my fighting had been done with my butt on the carpet. I decided to get up and throw a few punches on my feet. I mean, after all, my rear end was getting floor burns.

I got up, so did the guy with the ugly face, clawing at his tie, getting it loose. I belted him in the belly. He staggered back. I didn't want to knock him out, he had to take me to that hospital.

Besides, if I should kayo him and his buddy, Claudette Marly would insist I drag them out into the corridor and lock the door behind them. Then I was to drag—drag, ha!—her into the bedroom for some of that *flon-flon* she was talking about.

So I pulled my punches as I whaled out at him.

I drove him back over a chair. Man and chair hit the floor together. The guy with the splinters was on his feet now and sending out a fist in my general direction.

I blocked his blow.

I rammed him in the middle an inch above his belt buckle. He made sobbing sounds as he tottered backwards. Claudette was urging me to go after him, to finish him off.

I tried. I threw haymakers that would have rocked him sleepy-bye if they had landed. I made sure they did not. I followed him around the room, the wind of my near-misses blowing him ahead of me.

Pockmarked-face was up and diving for me.

His skull rammed into my hip, knocking me sideways. It was my turn to fall over a chair. We were making a shambles of the apartment all right. I caught him by his ears and twisted his head sideways so that it slammed into a wooden chest-leg. I rolled against him, sought for a wrestling hold.

I got a half nelson on his neck and head, but his body was bouncing around so savagely he broke the grip. His knee slammed my thigh. He was panting and puffing by this time, his face was scarlet and wet with sweat. I was in a little better shape but not by much.

Then something fell on my back, damn near breaking my spine.

The other guy, getting into the melee.

We bounced and bumped here and there. We upended an end table, we brought a standing lamp down over our threshing bodies, we even rammed into Claudette Marly and sent her flying.

Fists thudded into my jaw and belly. I figured I'd put up enough of a fight to make the Coxe Foundation proud of me. I would let them overpower me.

Hah! I had no say in the matter. Encouraged by their temporary success, the two bruisers went wild. They showered my face with knuckles. They turned my stomach-flesh black and blue.

I tried to tell them I was surrendering. They wouldn't have any part of that, they went on hammering away at the Damon features. Until they finally succeeded.

They knocked me cold.

CHAPTER THREE

My head hurt with something worse than the Excedrin headache the television screens make much of. I was strapped down on a cot, and could move neither my arms nor legs.

HECATE had me good.

My eyes still worked, however, so I studied the room in which I lay. It had white walls decorated with a couple of Picasso prints. Beside the cot where I was strapped down there was a dresser and a night table, plus a rocking chair. Austere quarters, but they were mine, all mine.

"Hoi!" I yelled.

The door opened. A nurse poked her head in and flashed a grin. The white cap perched on her neat black hair bobbed as she said, *"Bon jour, m'sieu.* I see we are ready to take our place in the world."

She came into the room, walking with a strut that made her breasts bounce enticingly behind her starched white uniform. No brassiere, but the necessary breastworks to fill a pair of C cups. There was amusement in her eyes as she reached to take my wrist between her fingers.

"I've heard you just about turned Claudette Marly inside out," she announced as she took my pulse. "The poor girl was hysterical when they carried you off."

"I have my moments," I grinned.

Her stare challenged me. I moved my shoulders in a little shrug. "I can't prove anything tied down like this," I suggested.

The nurse laughed, shaking her head. "Soon, maybe. Not right now. You've had an accident. A lamp fell on your head in Paris. You're here in Dampierre at a private hospital, being treated for a mild concussion."

"How'm I doing, everything considered?"

46

Her glance was enigmatic. "Everything considered, m'sieu, I'd say you were doing fine. Your pulse is normal. No more fever. Yes, you do very well, indeed."

"Then why don't I get up?"

"Plenty of time for that. A doctor must examine you first. So just lie back, rest, and be patient."

The doctor came in half an hour, a tall man, almost cadaverous in appearance, with a caved-in chest and a body as thin as a slat rail. His eyes were dark, ringed with purple flesh. His lips were thin, his Adam's apple prominent, and his voice was quite deep.

"*Bon, bon,*" he muttered, eyes glowing. "You are a very healthy specimen of manhood, m'sieu. You have thrown off the effects of the—of—ah—your blow, quite swiftly. I think you may be up and about, if you so wish."

I so wished, so in another half hour I was dressed in sports shirt and slacks—the hospital orderlies had secured a change of my clothes from the hotel—and was strolling down a hospital corridor. There were several nurses at a desk, eyeing me up and down. I gathered from their wide eyes and quick whispered confidences that Claudette Marly hadn't done my reputation any harm. I smiled at them, winked and passed on to the big French doors that opened onto a brick patio.

The air was brisk, fragrant with honeysuckle. I was a little puzzled at my apparent freedom, until I remembered that if the Coxe Foundation and old Walrus-moustache were right, I had a miniature bugging device in my skull that would theoretically, prevent any attempt to run away.

I played it cosy. I strolled about, drew deep lungfuls of perfumed air into my lungs, then went back into the hospital building like any good patient. I walked up to the nurse at the hall desk.

"How's chances of getting something to eat, honey?" I asked. "I'm starved."

Her smile was a yard wide. "*Certainment,* m'sieu! Your need for food is most understandable." The way she said it, it sounded like a dirty dig. I guess she was remembering Claudette Marly.

They served me ham and eggs, toast and coffee in my room. I was no sooner finished with my second cup than two men entered and stood staring at me. I pushed back the card table that held my dishes and cups, and stared back.

The men were above middle height, muscuar and lithe; they looked like athletes. Their skin was heavily tanned and they had a hard, ruthless look to their eyes. At first glance, I had thought them to be musclemen. Now I revised my estimate.

"Ah, the brains of the outfit," I murmured, and one of the men—slightly balding and with intense black eyes that seemed to crackle as he blinked—visibly started, turning to stare at his companion.

The second man merely smiled. He was suave, dressed with impeccable taste in a Pierre Cardin suit with all the elegant accessories. His hair was a reddish-blonde, worn rather long, and his eyes were a washed-out blue.

"Brains, Professor Damon?"

"Of this hospital, of course," I murmured, waving a hand about casually, The balding man quieted, seeming more at ease. "I assume you run it. I want to thank you for everything you've done. I just hope I can afford the bill."

"You can afford it, Professor—believe me," said Pierre-Cardin-suit. His smile was not nice as he added, "We've made sure of that. You see, Professor, you interest us very much."

"Oh?"

"Yes, indeed. As a matter of fact, many men and women all over the world interest us, here at HECATE." He chuckled at my expression. "Don't bother to put on an act, Professor. We know all about you and Rhea Carson, how you saved her life. And what you and your chief learned later at the Caldwell Neurosurgical Clinic."

I blinked at that all right, until I realized he was guessing. The fact that the man who had saved Rhea Carson's life had come so soon to France might be a building block on which to construct a whole set of theories.

His smile was very friendly. "That is usually how we select a great number of our operatives, from their past history, or because of their successful interference with our plans. Most organizations would kill their best opponents. Not HECATE."

Balding-man said softly, "We turn them to our ad-

48

vantage, we use them. It's an advantage we have over other organizations who utilize secret agents such as yourself. We are always sure of your obedience, always positive you will remain loyal to us."

Pierre-Cardin-suit nodded affably. "Permit me. This man with me is Doctor Cyrano Matelot, one of the world's foremost experts in the field of interacerebral electric stimulation. I am Doctor Yves Roger-Viollet." He was very modest about it. Yves Roger-Viollet was a name to rank with that of Clinton Thayer in the field of neurosurgery.

I rose and bowed. "It is my privilege, gentlemen," I told them, and meant it. I always admire brains and ability in a man, even in an enemy.

Roger-Viollet was very pleased. He rose and bowed also, as did Matelot. Apparently I was not being controlled by the buttons in my head at the moment, so what I had done was quite voluntary and they accepted it as a compliment.

"We shall get along, Professor," murmured Roger-Viollet.

Doctor Matelot muttered supiciously, "I don't think you understand the meaning of what you've just heard, Damon. Ours is an organization called HECATE. We have selected you to act as one of our secret agents."

I shrugged. "I also assume that you have placed electronic miniatures in my head, as you did with Rhea Carson. I am therefore under your direct control and supervision."

Hell, I might as well be honest with them. They knew my background and could guess at why I had come to Paris. I knew something about them. Why not put our cards on the table? I was playing this by ear, and my ear told me to do what I had done.

Yves Roger-Viollet regarded me thoughtfully. "You are either a very brilliant man, Professor—or a very stupid one."

I grinned, "Do I have a choice?"

"Not really," Matelot announced.

My hands went wide. "Then why fool around with words? I'm your man, whether I like it or not. I assume that while I work for you, I'll live high off the hog, as they

49

say in the American southland. Good food, good shelter, exciting women to bed down."

Matelot chuckled with ribald enjoyment. "I have heard how Claudine carried on when you were taken away from her. You must be a very efficient *courailleur,* Professor."

"I do all right."

Yves Roger-Viollet made a sudden motion with his hand. "Let me get this straight. You are a secret agent for an American organization. You came to Paris to investigate HECATE. Now that we have you in our power, you are quite willing to accept the fact? Without fuss and fury? Without putting up a fight?"

"Could I put up a fight?" I asked.

Matelot said, "No. Not in the least."

They did not know that a counter-button was hidden away somewhere inside my body, and that with its help I could break their electronic control over my brain any time I chose. It was my ace in the hole, my card up the sleeve. I kept my features to a poker face so as not to betray my thoughts.

"We may have selected better than we knew," muttered Doctor Roger-Viollet. "However, we shall soon know the answers to that. Professor, please come with us."

In the hallway outside my room, half a dozen muscular young men in tight black uniforms were waiting. I grinned at sight of them.

"In case I had put up a fight?" I wondered.

Roger-Viollet nodded. "To be sure. Ours is an efficient, foresighted operation. We try always to anticipate the possible."

The six guards fell into step behind us, the overhead lights reflecting off the silver crescents on their skin-tight blouses. I knew a little about the goddess Hecate, enough at least to understand that she was also known as Diana on Earth and Luna in the sky. A moon goddess, among other things, which would explain the crescent.

I said something of this and Matelot nodded.

"Hecate was a mysterious divinity," he explained. "Actually, she was three persons in one, Luna or Selene in the sky, Diana or Artemis on Earth, and Proserpina or Persephone in the underworld.

50

"She is represented by three bodies or three heads, or by the moon in one of its phases. She could send terrible demons from the lower world. She was a sorceress and the mother of all witchcraft. She was to be found wherever two roads intersected or near tombs or even where the blood of a murdered person had dripped onto the ground."

"A rather terrifying lady," I murmured.

"Indeed she was—and is, Professor."

"Okay, okay. I get the hint."

I was taken on a guided tour of the HECATE compound. There was the hospital and its attached laboratories, the gymnasiums where the patients exercised, a large swimming pool, and various assorted buildings. This was the public image.

Beyond the acre of lawn that surrounded the compound, there was a small forest. We walked along a narrow path between the trees for about half a mile. Then the real headquarters of HECATE came into view.

Three low buildings, windowless, were surrounded by a high wire fence that was flooded with enough electricity to kill any man or animal who might come in contact with it. Roger-Viollet touched a gadget on his belt and the metal gate swung back silently. We went through and it closed behind us. All very efficient, and designed to safeguard the privacy of the HECATE family.

The door of the nearest building opened as we approached. A girl guard in the same black-and-silver-crescent uniform of the male guards in the hospital, stood at attention. The skintight uniform blouse looked better on her than it had on the men. Ditto the hip-hugging tights and leggins.

I eyed her. She eyed me, choking back a smile at my swift perusal of her uniform and what was under it.

"This is operations headquarters," explained Matelot. "It is the brain of HECATE. I tell you this because we expect you to be one of our finest operatives, Damon. You might as well understand what it is you're a part of. Here we keep contact with our men all over the world. Here we receive information and send out orders."

And keep the files on those operatives, I thought.

"Beyond this building is our testing grounds," Roger-Viollet chimed in. "It is there we prove the ability of our secret agents—as you will be tested in a few days. We have a rating chart for each individual, based on fighting prowess, on sex ability, on perception of danger and reaction to obstacles. It is a thorough rating system. You shall be so rated."

We moved on to the testing grounds.

"We regret we cannot show you the testing mazes themselves, which are underground," Yves Roger-Viollet murmured. "No contestant can see them until the actual event. It might give him an unfair advantage."

What I was permitted to see was a room filled with what looked like giant computers. They had control panels inset into all the lower walls, with television screens above them. What transpired in the testing mazes could be seen and assessed here, corrections made, new dangers added or old ones removed during the course of the trial. It was a room of flawless metal walls and glistening data processing and mind-control machines. It was a little frightening in its efficiency. In here, I would be judged and found wanting, or accepted to full membership in HECATE. For my purposes, I wanted not only to be accepted, but to pass these tests with flying colors.

"You have three days of rest, Professor," Matelot smiled.

Then the tests.

The tour was over. We turned and marched out into the French sunlight. I was determined to give a good account of myself, not only for my individual reputation, but for the honor of the Thaddeus X. Coxe Foundation. I had done so many jobs for the Foundation I felt a lot of loyalty to it.

I spent the next three days in the gymnasium and in the outdoor swimming pool. I exercised, I worked until the sweat ran down off my six-foot-tall frame. I normally stay in perfect physical condition—my tasks for the Foundation see to that—but I figured to add an edge to my muscles by a steady honing.

Biggest sacrifice of all, I ignored the nurses. From time immemorial, warriors going off to war have abstained from sex. I considered that I was a warrior marching off to war, if the tests were to be anything like I imagined them to be. So I offered up my abstinence to Mars and hoped that Venus would be understanding.

I slept and ate like a child too.

On the morning of the fourth day, energy was bubbling in my every vein. I was awakened by a guardsman and told to come with him, dressed only in a bathrobe and slippers.

I paraded out of the hospital and along the walk toward the testing grounds with a dozen nurses staring after me. Just before I entered the woods, I turned and blew kisses back at them. They cheered and waved their handkerchiefs. At least I had somebody rooting for me.

I was marched through a hall of the headquarters building and conducted down a staircase to a metal door. The guardsman knocked. The door opened, revealing a long corridor, with a second metal door at its far end.

When this metal door opened, I found myself staring into what seemed to be a lounge room, with divan and matching chairs, pictures on the wall, magazines on a coffee table, an oriental rug underfoot. The guard motioned and I removed my bathrobe and slippers. I was stark naked.

The guard said, *"Bon chance, m'sieu!"*

The metal door clanked shut, locking me in.

I did not move. There was trouble here. I could sense it. My head told me this was the first test, this room. Something about it was damn dangerous. I squatted down, patting the rug, head cocked to listen. Nothing. I put a foot on the rug, gingerly testing my weight. No gas, no explosive.

I took another step, and another.

"Bon, bon!" said a voice. "You are no blunderer, Professor Damon. We are happy to see this. But we are not destroyers. We shall not trap you with hidden death—unless we give you a very obvious clue. The dangers you shall face, for the most part, will be quite apparent ones."

I figured HECATE did not want to kill me. That was reasonably obvious. But I was determined to rack up a good score on their marking sheets. I would do my own thinking, thank you, and the hell with their bland advice.

I was halfway across the rug when I saw it.

The glass on one of the large pictures above the divan was foggy. The room was warm, but not that warm, and

53

the air was not humid. Ergo, as the mathmeticians say, something like warm gas was coming into the room—and close to the picture.

I leaped onto the divan. I shifted the picture on its wiring. There was a hole in the wall behind it, out of which an odorless gas was pouring. I was naked. I had no cloth on me which which to plug it.

I glanced around the room. The coffee table!

Jumping down, I lifted the long, low table, got a grip on one of its legs, and snapped it off. I got back on the divan and rammed the small, lower end of the table leg into the hole, hard.

No more gas.

I heard somebody chuckle over the intercom.

The far door of the room opened invitingly. I accepted the invitation and walked through it into another room. The door did not close behind me. Maybe my examiners were giving me a chance to back out, if I wanted.

A wall of the room rose up. Three girl guardsmen stood there, just as naked as I was. Each of them had a bullwhip in her hand, however. Their faces did not look at all friendly.

Three whips came up and lashed out, with me as their target. I dived forward under those flying thongs and drove hard into the bare legs of the three girls. One of them yelped as her bare back banged into the metal barrier behind her.

A second girl tried to conk me with the butt of her whip.

The third girl was coiling her whip for another try.

I got a hand on a soft thigh of the second girl and my fingers bit in. She had no clothes on, so I had to get her into my flesh. I rolled under her so her belly got the bite yanked her down across me just as the whip started biting into my flesh. I rolled under her so her belly got the bite instead. She screamed in pain, doubling up.

I reached over her breastworks for the whip.

My fingers went around it. I tugged and the number three girl came tumbling forward. I erupted off the floor, driving the heel of my hand into her temple and slamming her other temple into the edge of the opened wall that had slid back to reveal them. She crumpled.

The girl who had yelped sent her lash at me.

I took it over my bent back as I got to my feet. The second girl was still conscious, so I gave her a karate chop on the neck an instant before I came up on my toes. She lay there motionless.

I had one opponent left.

She was a lush brunette, with quivering breasts and a belly that sucked in and out as she breathed. Her features were very attractive; all these HECATE honeys were good-looking, I was discovering. But attractive or ugly, the sight of her bullwhip roused something other than sex thoughts in my mind.

My back stung where she had lashed me. We circled each other as she coiled her whip for another crack at my nakedness. I let her coil it, let her throw her arm back and up for the blow.

I left my feet as if sliding for a base, feet out in front of me. My soles rammed her ankles, and she fell straight down on top of me.

I locked my arms about her and squeezed, holding her arms to her soft sides. Her body was slick with sweat, and as she writhed against my grip, it moved easily, giving me the benefit of hard breasts and soft loins against my nakedness.

My manhood responded with enthusiasm.

I saw startled awareness spring to life in the eyes staring down into mine, only inches away. The soft thighs moved, my pulsing phallus trapped between them.

I panted, "To the victor belongs the spoils, sweets!"

My fingers were sunk deep in her buttockflesh as I shifted her slightly and rose up, making her know the strength of my manhood. She cried out at the invasion and her fevered eyes glaring down at me softened slightly, as she accepted me fully.

She tried not to move, sought to free herself, but the hot blood was beating in my veins and I was not letting her go. My flesh needed the solace of her flesh; I was not finished with this obstacle course I was running; her flesh would renew mine, make me know I was a man, and enable me to act as a man should act.

I rolled her over, I hammered myself at her. She cried out harshly, she flung her head from side to side, but my

55

arms were about her slim middle and I kept her to her task until her rigidity melted and her long legs came up to lock about my waist.

My flailing hips bounced her buttocks off the floor, rode them back and forth and sideways. I heard a squishy sound above the cries her open lips were pouring out, the wet pull and tug of our united genitals. She was tossing her head back and forth, her belly muscles knotted and loosed as she rode her hips along with mine, everything forgotten but the delight in her female flesh.

I lasted a long time, as I always do. Even when her muscles went limp in the middle of a shrill scream, when her orgasmic spendings knocked her senseless, I was still in the throes of wild desire.

Pulling free, I left her sprawled with thighs widespread on the floor, turning to the other women who were just coming to, lifting their heads and looking dazedly around them. I stalked the nearest girl, my desire out there ahead of me.

Over the intercom I heard a woman pant, *"Mon Dieu! He is a horse! Look at him! Look at him!"*

My hand yanked the woman nearest me upward. She licked her lips, staring at my loins; her eyes were glazed, she was only half conscious. My arms went about her soft middle to fasten my fingers in her rump. I lifted her, thrust savagely.

She whimpered, but she took me.

I drove into her, backing her spine up against a wall in the suspended posture of the Hindu erotologists. She hung there, wailing softly in my ear, beaten, a conquered female fit only to be raped by the conqueror. Against my chest her breasts scratched deeply, her nipples swollen rigid. Her arms went about me, I could feel her coming alive in her female parts.

Back and forth, pound and push and pull, I made her know I was her superior. A kind of madness was in me at the moment; I was unthinking, a beast subject only to his flesh fury. My teeth fastened in her shoulder as I felt her shudder into her first orgasmic spasm, the pain of my teeth in her flesh adding to her erotic enjoyment.

There was a hand on my ankle. I took time off from my activities to glance down. The third woman was staring up

56

at us, licking her lips, clawing at my leg to raise herself upward.

She bit my thigh gently. Her tongue licked it. She was moving against my leg with jerky motions, rubbing her hard breasts against it. I got the feeling she might be something of a masochist, being left out of the sexual embrace yet stimulated by that very omission.

I reached down, caught her long brown hair, yanked her upward, cupped her middle with an arm, and kissed her. Her mouth was open, wet. Our tongues fought between our lips. Her mount was thrust against my thigh, she moved it against me in a frottage frenzy.

"Please," she begged. "Please. . . ."

"Bend over—against the wall!"

She broke away, turned and put her palms flat to the wall. Her rump thrust back, her white legs were spread wide. In my arms, the girl whose spine was rubbed raw against the wall gave a faint cry and loosened her grip on me.

I dropped her, swung to the other woman.

My body invaded hers, she sobbed as she felt my strength. I reached around her, caught her dangling breasts and squeezed them gently, even while I drove myself furiously. She stayed right with me through three convulsions. Not until her knees weakened, telling me they could no longer support her pleasure-drained body, did I sink with her, still moving.

I heard female voices crying out in awe and admiration over the intercom. The nurses? Were they here to watch, having heard all about Claudette Marly and me? I did not know, I didn't care.

I was the rat in the maze, being tested.

If they wanted to watch—let them!

The third woman was kneeling, moaning, finished with her share in my victory binge. I gave her soft buttocks a gentle pat, and got to my feet.

There was a red door in the far wall. I began my walk toward it and my next test. As I approached, the red door slid back.

I stepped into the neighboring chamber.

The red door slammed shut.

Instantly the metal floor fell away. Where the floor had

57

been was one vast blue flame leaping ceilingward. The heat was unbearable. Sweat ran from my every pore, naked as I was. In a few minutes, I would be baked alive. Nothing could live inside this room. Nothing!

I had to find the answer to this newest danger—fast!

Just below my toes was the opening out of which the blue flame jumped and danced. A meshwork of metal rods and burners had been concealed below the floor. Under the burners was a second series of metal rods that crisscrossed the area.

Heat rises. It would be hot under the flame, but not nearly so hot as it was in the room where I was being cooked.

I stepped forward and dropped like a stone.

My hands shot forward, caught at a metal rod. My muscles tightened, breaking my fall. I swung by the rod over black emptiness. It was not hot down there. A cool wind blew, and the rod itself was cool, almost cold to the grip of my fingers.

Hand over hand I moved along that rod until I was at the opposite wall. Apparently I triggered off a mechanism of some kind, because as I stretched an arm upward to grip the flooring, the blue frame died out.

"You have done well, Professor Damon. Extremely well. Now let us test your tolerance to pain." There was a chuckle. "We can usually learn the pain tolerance of our candidates before this, one way or the other. Your reactions have been so swift, your understanding of a situation so instant, that you've foiled our attempts to learn that tolerance point."

I was standing before a yellow door, facing it. The heat that was still in this room from the aftereffects of the blue flame was making me sweat, but I knew that beyond the yellow door there was another obstacle to be faced and overcome.

The yellow door slid back.

I moved forward into the room. A sword lay on the floor before me. It was not a regular sword, it was made of leather so that it was half a whip. I bent down, picked it up.

In my college days, I had been on the fencing team, so I knew an epee from a rapier. The sword I held here was very light to the touch, its leather blade whistling as I swung it.

A section of the wall swung back. A tall girl built like Juno, fully six-feet-two from the soles of her bare feet to the long black hair that hung down her back, was stepping into the room.

She carried a sabre; not the thickly bladed sabre of the cavalryman but the thinly bladed sabre of the modern-day fencer, a length of slim metal that could not cut but that could sting with the fury of a thousand scorpion bites when it landed on your flesh.

The girl would be a master fencer. I could tell that from the confident way she held her blade, from the ease of her manner. Left foot advanced, she came toward me, left hand dangling in the classic manner of the duelist.

I met her halfway, I parried her first three slashes. I tried to hit her with the leather blade I held, but she was too adroit for me.

A voice said, "Freeze him."

Another voice said, "No, no. We've never interfered yet during a test pattern. We couldn't get an honest score."

"But he's liable to get out of this one too!"

"Then his score will show it."

I was to be left on my own. They weren't going to radio-control me, the electrodes in my brain were not to be used against me.

There was no need for that.

The big black-haired Brunhilda came in at me, blade blurring, bare feet slapping the floor.

I lifted my blade to parry—

She was feinting. The sabre swept around my sword, slapping my thigh—and I damn near died.

Her steel blade was electrified. An electric shock ran through my naked body from my toenails to my topknot. My body jerked uncontrollably. The naked Valkyrie with the sabre laughed gleefully and drew back her sword to belt me again.

This time, instead of parrying, I leaped into the air. My body was not grounded now, and while the electricity ran through my flesh, it did not hurt.

For the brief moment I was up there in the air, my opponent was defenseless. I made the leather blade sing as I

59

whipped it right at her bouncing breasts.

Those big mammaries had been a distraction to me until this moment. Seeing them swing and sway, watching them bounce and bobble as she moved to the attack or leaped back, had sapped my concentration.

But now!

She screamed.

Mouth open, head thrown back, she let out a cry that would have done credit to a wounded banshee. Deep into her soft breastflesh went my leather blade, across each tender nipple until the heavy globes were indented a full inch.

She forgot her job, the sabre in her hand, and me. She bent over, dropping the sword and putting her hands to her hands to her agonized breasts. I was on the floor by this time, so I stepped to one side and whaled her across the backside.

I felt sorry for the girl but we were temporary enemies, and it was her or me. I whaled her behind a second time and then as she ran, I brought the leather whip-blade up between her bare thighs.

Her body bucked and jumped. Her screams raised the hairs on the back of my neck. She drove forward into the wall, a hand covering her crotch, her forearm across her throbbing breasts.

My dark Brunhilda crouched there, whimpering, bent almost double. Her big black eyes were fastened on my face in piteous appeal.

"Don't hit me again. Please! Please! No more."

I still held the leather sword. I swung it a couple of times and asked the air, "Well? What about it?"

"This one is incredible," somebody said.

"We'll have to weaken him for the next trap. Professor Damon!"

"I hear you," I muttered, staring at the big girl bent above her purpling breasts, holding them in her palms, crooning to them.

"Take her!"

The girl looked up in blind horror. It dawned on me suddenly that she might be a Lesbian, that she hated men, that she reveled in the idea of using that electrified sword against them.

I felt a surge of cruelty touch my senses. I realized that her bosses knew and appreciated what she was, that this was a way to punish her for having failed them. Ordinarily I am gentle and tender with a female. Now the electrodes in my brain were throbbing, sending out their commands.

I leaped, catching her wrist, yanking her sideways and along the metal floor. With my free hand, I gripped her flowing black hair, dragging her that way, so that she cried out in her torment.

Against a wall I flung her so that she sprawled before me, her heavy thighs wide apart. The swollen lips of her femininity must have hurt like hell, but they were my target. I could have fought the radio commands, but I did not dare let the HECATE leaders know about the counter-stimulators hidden in my body.

I flung myself upon her, ripe for rape.

My hands caught her breasts, squeezing them tightly. She tried to put up a fight, but there was no spirit left in her. My fingers pained her as the leather swordblade had. She rose up to throw me off, but that only aided my intentions.

She was a virgin.

Her mouth opened as she screeched to my penetration, she bucked and writhed beneath me. A moment only was I halted, then I surged forward to this ultimate conquest. She lay limply beneath me, her eyes were squeezed shut and her lips were twisted as if in a cataleptic trance.

Tears came out from beneath her lashes.

I was no longer Rod Damon, founder of the League for Sexual Dynamics, I was only a male robot geared to obey whatever hand was sending out those orders to me. My body thrust and drove. I was a remote-controlled maniac, without thought, without reason, only with the animal side of me commanded to function as a male.

Hate blazed at me from the black eyes below me. Hate whispered to me silently between her twisting lips. I reminded myself that she was under the control of HECATE just as much as Rhea Carson had been and even more than I was. She would have gloried in her triumph had she been able to being me to my knees groveling and begging as she had brought every other candidate with whom she had fought her one-sided duel.

And yet, none of this mattered to me. Only in some dim corner of my mind did I have these thoughts. All the rest of me was a male monster commanded to do its will on the female of the species.

And do the will of my master, I did.

For ten minutes, for half an hour. My flesh was indefatigable. I was a true automaton. I heard voices crying out over the intercom as hidden eyes watched me and marveled. My satyrism was no longer a personal thing, it was a weapon in the hands of HECATE. And HECATE used it to punish this female swordsman for her inability to defeat me.

When the electrodes stopped sending their commands, I fell away from my inert antagonist. I lay on my back and gulped in air through my open mouth. Slowly sanity came back to me.

I had performed nobly. I knew that. I had done what HECATE wanted of its initiates, I had been everything I had expected of myself. I waited for some sort of congratulatory message from the intercom. There was none, just the sudden throbbing of the electrodes that told me I had another task waiting for me.

I got up and walked toward the green door.

My hand turned the doorknob and I stepped through into a room filled with a soft white light. There was a big green jewel hanging inches below the ceiling, far out of my reach.

I studied the green stone. It was a chunk of aquamarine, the largest I had ever seen, although I was vaguely recalling that some years back, a gigantic slab of this greenish stone had been found in Brazil and that it now reposed in a New York City bank. That gem had weighed upwards of fifty pounds.

The one that hung in the air above my head was nowhere near that big. This one could have weighed ten, maybe fifteen pounds. But I gathered its size was of no importance.

"Professor Damon," said a voice.

"I'm listening."

"The aquamarine you see above you. Do you think you can get it down from there? It hangs by magnetic force —two iron plates have been affixed to its sides while powerful electromagnets grip them to keep it motionless."

"Anybody got a ladder handy?" I asked.

"No ladder, nothing but your naked self, Professor. It's a test of wits, if you want to look at it that way."

The ceiling was twelve feet above the floor, which was carpeted with what seemed to be an oriental rug, laid wall to wall. I am six feet or so tall. This left a good four and a half feet between my extended arm, raised over my head, and the aquamarine. Not being a kangaroo, I couldn't jump that high.

Some test of wits!

I walked around the room, studying the stone. I could make out the iron plates now. They had been painted green to camouflage them. The electromagnets would hold those plates forever, unless I could come up with a way to dislodge the aquamarine.

It would not need much of a tug to knock it out of the magnetic pull that held it. If I were seven feet tall and could jump like a pro basketball player, I could leap up, slap it with a hand and send it flying.

I was not seven feet tall. I could not jump like Wilt Chamberlain. But I could use a wall as a springboard.

I ran for the nearest wall, leaped high. I put my bare feet against the cool plaster and took off from that solid foundation with a leap. I held my hand extended out as far as it would go.

My straining fingertips went under the aquamarine, missing it by six inches. There wasn't enough kangaroo blood in me, I guess. Still, I didn't give up. I kept jumping at that wall and bouncing off it like a rubber ball. I narrowed the six inches to maybe four, but it just wasn't enough.

I sat down on the carpet to have a think.

There were some assets I had: a good, muscular body and a brain that sometimes came through in a pinch when I put pressure on it. I let my eyes roam about the room. I felt convinced the answer to my problem was in here with me. HECATE would play fair in this regard, anyhow. It would supply what I needed.

Of course! I was sitting on the answer.

The carpet! All I had to do was roll it and use it like a

63

long arm. It would more than reach up to the stone and knock it out of the magnetic field.

Nice thinking, Damon! I congratulated myself.

There was only one thing wrong with my idea. The carpet was glued to the wooden floor below it. I couldn't so much as lift a half-inch of the stuff. I sat back on my naked rump and thought some more.

The rug was here for a purpose. HECATE did nothing in this testing maze without a reason. But what the hell good was a rug I couldn't lift? Think, Damon! Use that gray matter that earned you the rank of professor at a big-time university. The aquamarine, the rug beneath your behind, the stark bare walls.

They all added up to an answer.

My rump ached and itched. I moved it to a different position. And then it came to me, the solution to my problem. It was so simple, I began to laugh. I lay back on my spine and let the peals of mirth ring out.

A voice rasped, "You find it amusing, Professor?"

"Very," I managed to gasp when I could.

On my feet again, I walked to the wall and stared up at that segment of it opposite the aquamarine. Carefully my eyes went over it, and now I could make out the faintest of hairline markings in the plaster. Part of that wall was metal, the grid plate for the electromagnet hidden behind it. Whatever hand had painted the wall this pallid ivory had tinted the grid plate the same color, so it was almost invisible. A masterly job. A man had to stand a certain way to take notice of that plate.

I turned away from the painted plate. I could reach it with a reasonable jump, I needn't be seven feet tall to do it. The plate extended down the wall almost within hand-reach.

Now I moved back and forth over the rug, letting my feet rub its material. I had only my naked body, but the human body is capable of storing and then releasing static electricity. And by moving my feet back and forth over this rug, I could work up a reasonably good amount of it.

Over the intercom a woman whispered, "He knows!"

I waited until I practically began to tingle before I made my run. I leaped up off the rug, I flicked my fingertips out toward the grid plate. I could see sparks as my fingernails touched the painted metal.

The contact stung. My body received a mild electric shock. But the aquamarine came tumbling down to hit the floor and bounce. Apparently HECATE had geared its hidden magnet to shut off at even a minute amount of electricity coming in contact with the grid plate.

I picked up the aquamarine and held it high.

"Now what?" I asked.

There was a little silence. I gathered that somebody had shut off the relay switch that sent sound from the control room down into the maze. They were talking about me up there, they were wondering what in the hell to do about me. I got the notion that they felt I was out-thinking them.

Hell! I was.

The intercom system squawked, then quieted. A voice rasped into life. "You are something of an eye-opener, Professor Damon. We must admit you have passed all our tests with more than a little to spare. Isn't there anything you can't do?"

I figured that was a rhetorical question. I didn't bother answering it. HECATE was not finished with me. There was more to come.

"If you will please walk through the orange door, Professor?"

A section of wall opened. I saw the orange door.

The orange door opened as I stepped before it. I stared into a large chamber in which the only object was a huge X, a wooden cross set on its ends in the shape of a cross of Saint Andrew. I moved into the room as the green door closed, leaving me alone.

I waited, but nothing happened.

Then metal whispered as five doorways opened in the walls. Five naked girls came leaping out, right at me. I whirled to face two of them, who slid to a halt. The other three hurled themselves at me.

As I turned to face two of these girls, the third one hit the back of my neck with the edge of her hand in a karate blow. I staggered forward. One female grabbed my right arm, another tackled the left. They made their bodies dead weights.

65

I sank the fingers of my hands into female flesh, but the girls only grunted and hung on tighter. By this time the remaining three were slamming me with the edges of their hands. I rocked back, I tried to fight them off, but it was as if the electrodes had command of my body. I could only stand there and take it.

My vision blurred under those blows. I felt numb around my neck, and there was a roaring in my ears.

I stood there suspended between two girls, swaying slightly, all but out on my feet. Then soft female hands dragged my unresisting body to the Saint Andrew's cross. I was lifted and held face down against that X by four girls as the third one clicked manacles about my ankles and about my wrists so that I hung suspended there.

"We are sorry about this change in plans, Hecate-Hero Damon, but your stubborn refusal to be overcome by any of our traps has necessitated a change in plans.

"Before we turn these girls loose on you, we wish to let you know that you have passed every test with flying colors. Your score is perfect; you have rated higher than any other operative we have.

"We are proud to accept you as a member of the team. But first we are determined to learn your threshold of pain endurance, your tolerance to all methods and means of torment. If it helps you any to know you are the first candidate ever to reach this position, be solaced by the information.

"Go ahead, girls."

The girls were drooling to go ahead. They were pretty females, extremely shapely, with all the necessary feminine equipment of firm breasts, handsome legs, lean bellies, dark or light patches of pubic hair that matched their long tresses.

One of them moved in on me, placing a footstool directly beneath my parted thighs. My male apparatus hung down inches from her face as she sat there. Up came her hands to caress and stroke and fondle. Within seconds that part of me was upstanding and at attention.

A second girl—a blonde honey—went around behind me and began to spank me with a wooden paddle. The blows did not hurt, at first; they stung my flesh and roused my male desires, but there was no pain. Not until the

66

blonde put down the paddle and reached for a Russian knout. The girl on the footstool had gotten into the act again, she held a small bamboo rod that she kept flicking against me gently, punishing my male apparatus.

The bamboo stung. It sent stabs of agony throughout my system. My middle arched and swung to avoid those easy blows. I say easy, because if they'd been any harder, they would have injured me permanently. As it was, I began to groan; I couldn't help it. Harder blows would have made me scream.

The honey blonde began on my bare backside with the knout. The true Russian knout is a deadly thing, there are pieces of jagged metal inserted into the knots that dot its cords. This was an imitation, of soft leather specially treated so as not to break the skin.

There was pain, however, a hell of a lot of pain. I hung there shuddering, biting my lips, moaning softly. Every time the knout hit me, the girl between my thighs would ready her bamboo rod and hit me while the female behind me was coiling her knout for another blow.

My beating went on and on.

The other three girls came forward. One girl, a brunette, carried a black leather pouch. She stood before my straining manhood, smiling as she dipped her hand into the pouch. Her cupped palm emerged, holding a heap of powder tinted red, of the type, I assume, with which Hai-men Ch'ing anointed his own organ in the Chinese classic, *Chin Ping Mei*.

This powder she began patting onto my swollen flesh. I felt the effect almost at once. The red stuff stung. The combination of stinging powder on my manhood, the bamboo rod beating me where I was most sensitive, and the knout cutting into my buttocks, drove me crazy. I thumped my body against the Saint Andrew's cross, I fought the manacles until my wrists and ankles were bleeding.

Somewhere, a woman was sobbing. It took me several minutes to realize that her sobs were coming over the intercom. Whoever was watching what the five girls were doing to me was becoming affected by it.

The room began to reel before my eyes. I had reached my pain tolerance level, all right; I was getting dizzy.

Everything was going around and around.

But no. It was the X that was moving. A mechanism was tilting it parallel to the floor with me still fastened to it. I lay on my back now—they must have freed and turned me over while I was unconscious—the manacles no longer pained me since my weight was supported by the crossbars.

Nobody was whipping me any more.

The cross was being lowered until I lay about two feet above the floor. My five tormentors came to stand on both sides of me, with one of them directly between my thighs. Each girl held a rattan fly-swatter. They began beating on my legs, the girl between my thighs was using her swatter against my genitals. Slowly the swatters worked, then faster.

I would not beg. I bit into my lower lip with my teeth until I drew blood but I would not beg. My body tried to squirm but the strength was all gone out of it.

Then the fly-swatters were tossed aside and the girls knelt down. They began kissing me, one my lips, another my throat, a third my nipples, a fourth my belly, the fifth my private parts. I could smell their perfumed flesh, the musky odors of their excited femininities. The hands and lips adoring my manhood was an added aggravation.

I could not help it. My lips parted, I shouted out an unintelligible sound that was a combination bellow of pure pain and a cry of unsatisfied lust. Never in my memory was my flesh so desirous of sexual satisfaction. The girls were rubbing their swollen breasts against me, leaning over me, their pretty faces smiling down at me in the lewd grin of the excited female with a man to play with, to arouse and refuse.

I thought, Is every woman HECATE employee a man-hater? Do they all get their kicks from teasing a male until he goes crazy with frustration? My body was bouncing up and down, my straining excitement was a monstrous mace demanding relief.

From somewhere far away a bell sounded.

The five females drew back, away from me. Now, I could see sexual tension in their faces, and I understood that they would have liked nothing better than to throw themselves on me and take the manhood that was almost bursting with its need. The naked girls padded toward their doorways, their nude behinds jiggling as if in protest to the electrodes in their brains which they were obeying.

The five doors slid shut.

I was alone in a rage of lust, in an agony of frustration. It was the worst of all the tortures.

CHAPTER FOUR

I was in hell. My body ached, it hurt, it demanded fleshly satisfactions. I could only lie there and suffer.

If I ever got out of this fix, I would kill every HECATE man or woman I could lay hands on. They were not testing me, they were torturing me to death because I was a Coxeman. My body flopped this way and that to seek respite from the torment in which I lay bathed.

"Professor Damon!" a voice cried.

"I hear you—damn you!" I growled.

A voice chuckled, "We must apologize, Professor. Your test turned out completely differently than we had anticipated. We have been unfair to you but we will try to make amends."

"Well, what are you waiting for?" I yelled. "Make them, make them! I'm dying, dammit."

Again came that soft chuckle. "Observe, Professor!"

The pain was gone. Intense pleasure had taken its place. I lay there in a spell of unendurable delight. My pleasure centers were being affected by the radio commands and electrical impulses penetrating into my brain. I was not a human being, I was a guinea pig being rewarded for a good performance, as the clever monkey gets the banana, I was getting my pleasure centers titillated. I lay there in a semi-trance, a beatific grin on my face, and reveled in ecstasy.

I do not know how long I lay insensible to anything but a mental nectar which I drank as a thirsty man gulps water. I could not get enough of it. I cared about nothing but the joys I was receiving. Five hours? Ten hours? I felt like a good Mohammedan who had died and gone to the houri heaven Mahomet had promised to his followers.

Even such things must end.

A doorway slid open and a nurse entered the room. Gently she unfastened the manacles and quite tenderly she assisted me off the wooden crossbars.

I said, "Come on back to my room with me, pussycat. I'm in the mood for love, as the song says."

"Later," she said, smiling and taking my left arm and most of my weight across her shoulders. "Your body's been through a lot today. We mustn't strain it."

I stared down at myself. I no longer had any excitement in my loins, I felt numb there, as if I were a eunuch. I told myself that maybe my pleasure centers needed a rest. No sense in overdoing things.

The nurse was joined by a male orderly on another floor and side by side they got me back to my little cubicle and into bed.

"Sleep," said the nurse bending over to kiss my forehead.

I wanted to grab her wrist and pull her under the covers. I was too weak for that, so I did what she told me. I slept.

Twelve hours later, a different nurse was in my room. She was busy setting out a Pierre Cardin suit, a Hathaway shirt, English boots and silk underwear, all for me. As she moved around, I watched her unbrassiered breasts shake and bounce. I still felt nothing except annoyance.

"Are you sure they didn't castrate me?" I worried.

Her laughter was spontaneous. "HECATE never castrates its males. HECATE never knows when their maleness will be needed in the interests of HECATE."

"Well, that's good to know."

I threw back the covers and started out of bed. The nurse smiled gently. "You're on a case right now. You have no time—nor ability—for anything else."

"You don't know me," I bragged, but apparently she did. I hugged and kissed her, but it was like hugging and kissing a straw woman.

"All right, all right, I'm still feeling the effects," I admitted. "What do I do now?"

"You go to the office."

I got dressed and went to the office. Yves Roger-Viollet was sitting behind a desk, waiting for me. Cyrano Matelot was not in sight. Doctor Roger-Viollet got to his feet, came around the corner of the desk and shook hands with me.

"You are going to be a most welcome addition to our organization, Professor," he told me.

"I seem to be in a blue funk, sexually. What'd you do to me? And when do I go back to normal?"

"Just as soon as you kill a man."

"Good. Let's get it over with so I can go back to doing my thing. It isn't any fun being like this."

"At once, Professor. At once."

Roger-Viollet reached into a desk drawer and brought out a Luger automatic. It was of blued steel, a perfect specimen of the handiwork of Hugo Borchart and Georg Luger. The automatic Roger-Viollet was handing to me across his desk was the 1917 model, fitted with the eight-inch barrel used by machine gunners in the first World War.

I took the gun into my hand, then glanced inquiringly at the HECATE leader. "Who do I use this on? And when?"

Roger-Viollet said, "The man you are to assassinate is Henri Planget."

"The NATO man?" I asked incredulously.

"Exactly! He has angered HECATE by working with the North American Treaty Organization despite our repeated warnings to back out. His death will teach other malcontents a lesson."

I nodded. It made no nevermind to me who they picked out as my victim, I did not intend to kill him anyhow. So I let Yves Roger-Viollet go on saying his piece without interruption.

"There is to be a summit meeting of NATO brass in Brussels. Planget will fly there to attend. He is staying now at the Chateau Frontenac on the Rue Pierre Charron. It is best he die in Paris, walking out of his hotel."

"And the manner and means of the assassination?"

Yves Roger-Viollet waved a casual hand. "These details I leave to you. You will naturally make certain that you are not captured. We don't want to lose any of our operatives. Since you are an experienced secret agent, you will have your own modus operandi. HECATE never interferes with such personal idiosyncrasies. We believe an experienced man like yourself will work better if he is more or less on his own."

This was a relief. It meant that I would not be under constant surveillance by HECATE while carrying out my job. I could come and go as I liked, I could pretend to carry out the assassination assignment, but never go through with it. I heaved a sigh of relief as I accepted a brown leather shoulder holster and strap from the doctor. I removed the Pierre Cardin jacket, fitted on the holster, slid the Luger into it. I put the coat on, shifted my shoulders for a better fit, and announced I was ready to travel.

Yves Roger-Viollet smiled his approval at my businesslike manner. He lifted out a packet of ten-thousand-franc notes, tossing them to me. "For your expenses. We treat our agents to the finest standard of living known. They never want for anything. As an instance, you'll find a Lamborghini Miura outfitted and ready for your use, close by the front gate. Until further notice, the Miura is your own."

All my clothes were still at the Plaza Athénée. All I need do is drive the Lamborghini Miura from Dampierre through Versailles into Paris. If anyone asked, I could say I'd been on a few days holiday in the countryside. Roger-Viollet assured me no one would bother asking, that visitors came and went, and the hotel staffs in Paris were trained never to ask embarrassing questions.

Half an hour later I was in the Lamborghini Miura doing sixty miles an hour along the highway. The Miura was fire-engine red, boasted a twelve-cylinder rear engine and was capable of a hundred and eighty miles an hour. It was a beautiful machine. I told myself it was just the sort of thing a secret agent should drive while on assignment.

The car drew whistles of appreciation through the traffic-crowded streets. I sat behind the wheel as if born to such luxury. If I had to get out of town in a hurry, this brain-child of Italian engineer Ferruccio Lamborghini was the perfect getaway vehicle.

I tossed the hotel doorman a hundred-franc note and told him to stable my car in the garage. He took the car himself, rather than giving it to an assistant.

Halfway through the lobby of the Plaza Athénée, I felt eyes devouring my body. I let my eyeballs roll around for

73

a while until I located a woman in a black satin cocktail gown, with a rope of pearls at her soft throat and a pearl bracelet on her arm, seated with crossed legs, smiling invitingly in my direction.

I sidestepped a bellhop and found myself in front of the lady in pearls. I bowed from the waist. "Countess! How good to see you again! It's been such a long time since the Grand Bahama party."

Her smile was sly, her blue eyes narrowed under false black eyelashes. "You are generous, m'sieu," she breathed, extending her ringed hand for me to kiss. "I wondered whether you would know me."

"How could I not know you?" I replied, wondering who the hell she was. She knew me, I felt intuitively that she did, and moments later she confirmed my notion when she rose and took my arm.

"We shall dine together, M'sieu Damon. And after that, you shall entertain me," she announced, letting my thigh know the skirted softness of her own.

She was enveloped by Chanel perfume, and the cocktail gown was cut low between her breasts so an onlooker—and I onlooked, believe me—could see the pale inner slopes of plump, quivering breasts. She was sex appeal *ne plus ultra,* a walking invitation to venery.

I was determined to accept her invitation as a kind of reward to myself for having passed the HECATE tests so successfully. I guided her toward the dining room, I ordered her pheasant under glass, I wined her on Sazerac cocktails.

The liquor did nothing for me. My companion was just as attractive as she had been when I crossed the lobby, but no more so. I did not engage in mentally undressing her, I did not reach out with a hand to toy with her fingers, I did not reach for her knee with mine. I did nothing at all. I was like a dead man.

I told myself I was imagining things.

This had never happened to me. If I were across a dinner table from a bedable female such as this Madame Margot Metayer, usually I was already half under the covers with her. And Mme. Metayer had beddytime play in mind. Her pointed pump caressed my ankle, slid up and down my shin. But I felt absolutely dead where it counts.

Oh, I was entertaining enough—with my tongue. I talked of the Riviera, of the blue movies I had seen, of Capri and Miami Beach. I made her laugh, I made her full red mouth quiver in anticipation.

But I was only half alive. I told myself not to worry, everything would turn out aces. I would be turned on as soon as I saw her without her dress.

And yet—

The memory of the nurse back at the HECATE Hospital worried me. I had not yanked her skirt up or pulled her into bed. Suppose HECATE had forbidden me any yack-yack until my job was over? I sat there, horrified. It could not be! Even HECATE would not be so tyrannical. And yet come to think of it, Roger-Viollet had said I would be a man as soon as I had killed Henri Planget. Could that be true?

I would find out in a little while, however. Mme. Metayer was reaching for her suede pocketbook and her gloves. Soon we would be in an elevator, rising to my suite of rooms.

I crowded her across the dining room, I brushed my loins against her girdled buttocks, hoping for some sign on life in my gonads. I stood close to her soft thigh as we waited for the elevator, gently moving my hips. Hidden by the people crowding in around us, I even ran my palm across her buttocks, down where the girdle did not reach.

There was a secret little smile on her lips all this while, as if she dreamed of things to come. Once she drew her hand across my front, and frowned when she found I was as limp as a dish-rag.

"Is anything wrong?" she murmured, penciled eyebrows arched.

My smile was weak. "Of course not. I am—er—but recently out of the hospital, but I'm in perfect health."

Her enigmatic eyes regarded me. She let her ripe red mouth smile, and gave a little shake of her head. "I could not have been mistaken. At the hospital in Dampierre? In the maze with those girls, one after another, it *was* you?"

The elevator halted, the doors slid back.

Mme. Metayer and I walked along the thick carpeting. I

75

asked, "How can you know about the maze test patterns? Are you one of the HECATE crowd.

Her laughter was soft. "*Mais non!* I was a watcher, a voyeur. Myself and several other married ladies were given permission to watch and observe your reactions under certain stimuli. It was most entertaining."

A ringed hand patted mine. "It left me an insatiably lustful state. I hope you can take care of it."

I sure hoped I could. If I couldn't, it meant—but I wouldn't think of that awful possibility. She went by me with a swish of her rounded hips, a rustle of her slip, a flirtatious cocking of her penciled eyebrows. By this time, with all these indications of intimacy, I should have been in a state of rigid expectation, enjoying a merry-go-up. But I was still a dishrag.

I caught Margot Metayer in my arms, I took her mouth between my lips and battened on it. Against my muscle-hardened body her large breasts and mounded belly made soft cradles that would have been stirring and arousing at any other time. I held the kiss for a long time.

When we surfaced for air, her face was dark with suspicion. "They've worn you out, those girls!" Contemptuously she flicked a forefinger against my manhood. "You see? You are *non sunt*—eunuchized!"

I reminded myself I was a practicing sexologist, the founder of the League for Sexual Dynamics. It did me no good. I was eunuchized, as the woman said. I was no good to her, I was a flabby fancy. I knew who to blame, it was HECATE in command of my brain. My amygdala, to be specific, the seat of all sexual desire.

Then I saw a glimmer of hope.

I had a counter-stimulator sewn somewhere in my body. It sent out impulses that counteracted the impulses from the HECATE control room. All I had to do was concentrate. The HECATE impulses only impelled, they did not compel my actions.

I grinned at Mme. Metayer, I lifted her in my arms and carried her about the room. "*Non sunt*, am I? I'll show you how *non sunt* I am! Just get ready for the greatest ride you've ever had, pussycat."

I tossed her on the divan in the living room. Her black cocktail dress flew back to show her handsome legs in gun-metal stockings and the bare thighflesh above them, bisected by her garters.

I knelt beside the divan, I kissed her soft thighs up and down, I licked them with my tongue. I became the proper philemaphile, someone who is very fond of kissing. I heard her cry out softly as she wriggled and writhed, letting her skirt slide back until I saw quite clearly that she wore no panties, just a black girdle that hid nothing from view except the tops of her plump buttocks and the lower curve of her belly.

I kissed her upper thighs as she moaned and quivered. I knew what she wanted me to do, I had no objections, I have been a cunniphilmiast in the past, with attractive women, and I saw no reason to make an exception of Madame Metayer. I let my mouth rove sideways past her taut garter. Her flesh was perfumed, inviting.

"Oui," she gasped, letting her thighs widen. *"Faire minette!"*

I *faire minetted,* putting every ounce of yearning into the play of lips and tongue. She was gasping, her head moving back and forth against the divan cushions. Her thighs were warm against my cheeks as she tightened them while her hand moved over my head caressingly.

She was in a state of ecstasy, mouth open and wailing, eyes wide but blind as they stared at the ceiling. Her hips shook, she cried out thickly, she drove herself at me.

"Now? Please, now?" she whimpered.

Her fingers pushed me back and away. She lay there with her dress twisted at her girdled hips. Her eyes blazed with desire. "Hurry, strip. *Mon Dieu,* don't tease me any more. Strip and come into me."

I wished that the floor might open up for me. I was not excited. I was a *chapon.* Yet my hands went to my Pierre Cardin jacket, thrust it off, revealing my holstered Luger at which her eyes grew enormous. I slipped out of the shoulder-apparatus, shirt and shorts.

Naked, I stood beside the divan, giving her proof that I was not in control of myself. HECATE was too powerful for the counter-stimulator in my body. No matter what I did, no matter how I feasted my eyes on the splayed white thighs and damp garden before me, I was useless.

I could have wept.

Mme. Metayer just lay there, smiling coldly. "Put your clothes back on," she muttered angrily. *"Tu est epuise!* You're finished."

It had occurred to me I was playing at bigger stakes than just pleasing this Frenchwoman. If I could not pleasure her body because of the radio controls in my head—I could not refuse to assassinate Henri Planget!

I saw her reach out with her hand to fondle my manhood. Her face had a disbelieving, stubborn look. She had seen me perform in the HECATE test trials, taking one girl after another, and she could not understand how I could be so pooped. My body was healthy, muscular. I liked girls. There was no reason to be impotent.

Her head closed in on my loins and she kissed me.

"Do you want to play games? Is that why you are so reluctant? You have a preference? Is it young girls? Does my body appear too old?"

"Of course not! You're a very attractive woman. I adore you. Your thighs are pleasure pillars to wrap my hips in as you trapped my head. I tell you—it's just a momentary weakness. You must believe me."

Even then, I hoped.

Mme. Metayer came off the divan with a flash of bare thighs. She stood beside me, bending to lift her dress up over her head, showing me her girdled hips, her navel, the bare expanse of midriff. Her breasts in the sheer brassiere she affected were *pommes d'amour.* Love apples. They were large and soft, quivery flesh half hidden behind black lace. I could make out the large brown nipples standing stiffly.

She let her cocktail dress drop from her fingers. Her red mouth was a curving delight as she blew my loins a kiss. In girdle and brassiere she moved around the room, dimpling a smile at me.

"You like the parade? You like to watch the woman walk about? *Voilà!* Watch me."

She was an erotic carving in her high-heeled shoes, moving back and forth like a Minsky stripteaser. Her ringed hands went to the clasps of her brassiere and her fingers worked a moment, then let the bra straps drop. Hunching her shoulders, she let the cups slide away from her dangling breasts.

78

Those breasts were big, white, and heavy. They would have roused a Nestor to a priapic frenzy as they shook and bobbled when she threw back her shoulders and shimmied at me. But me? I was still a *chapon!*

Mme. Metayer came closer until her nipples were stabbing my chest. Her hands were between us, toying, teasing. Glittering eyes half concealed by long black lashes challenged my manhood. Like me, she could not believe that I was incapable of erection.

I groaned, "It's no use. My stay in the hospital left me too weak to do anything. But, please, perhaps my tongue will be so 'eloquent' that you won't wish anything else."

"Liar," she laughed softly. "I saw you in action, remember? I know what you can do. When these five naughty girls went out and left you all alone—with your *fax* so delightfully enlarged—I thought I would rush down and take you while you were still on that cross. *Peste!* I'm sorry I didn't, now."

She looked down at me and sighed.

I knew I would never be able to pleasure her until I'd killed Henri Planget. I also knew that I was going to be forced to kill Henri Planget. HECATE had found the counter-stimulator and removed it.

I no longer had my ace in the hole. I was defenseless against the murder I must commit. There were bitter ashes on my tongue.

My hands itched to push away this woman who was determined to seduce me. I needed no seducing, normally; right now I was not normal. I was a robot, an automaton. I was good for one thing only, to put a bullet into a man and kill him.

My condition was not her fault. She wanted *danser*, and I wasn't able to give it to her. I passed my hands about her body, drew her against me, kissed her soft mouth. From her lips my mouth fell to her soft throat, to the upper bulges of her breasts, to her stiff nipples. She moaned as my mouth kissed them.

"Oh, yes," she panted above my head. "Do me that way!" As a sexologist I realized she was undergoing *theletage,* that excitement in a woman which is caused by the titillation of her nipples. Her soft palms cupped my cheeks, shifting me steadily from one breast to another.

79

After a time, her hips began to move.

She was sobbing in ecstasy as my hands pushed down her black girdle, unfastening the zipper and sliding the black lastex past her buttocks, baring her belly and the thick black pubic hair. Her hips were engaged in that undulating motion that so closely parallels the actual thing. Her eyes were closed tightly, her mouth was open.

"If only you could, if only you could," she kept whispering.

"Close your eyes," I murmured. "Pretend!"

She stood bent over, breasts hanging.

"Don't move," I warned.

In my valise, I had a number of sexual curiosities I had picked up in Paris before setting out on my trip with Claudette Marly. Even on my assignments as a Coxeman, I am still the L.S.D. founder. One of these curiosa was an imitation penis formed from hard rubber, also tinted in flesh tones. The second was an artificial vagina of flesh-tinted fabric. The third was a phallatic splint.

I stood behind Madame Metayer and fitted the splint over my limp flesh. In these hollow splints, there is a space to cram the living flesh. I fitted myself into it and leaned forward.

She screamed as I entered her, screamed and bucked and jounced her hips in a side to side movement that would have delighted me at any other time. I reached around and caught her dangling breasts, fastening them in my palms by tightening my fingers. Then I let my hips go crazy.

Our union went on and on.

Until her knees buckled and she fell forward. I dropped with her, cushioning her body. She finished with a savage wrench of her hips and a thick cry of utter satiety. Then she lay boneless, almost unconscious.

I drew away, angry at myself, disgusted at my performance. I felt I had prostituted my position in order to give this Frenchwoman temporary satisfaction. I got to my feet, undoing the splint.

Mme. Metayer opened her eyes.

She stared in horror at the apparatus I had used on her. Sick dismay touched her face and her hand lifted as if to push away the sight.

80

"*Batarde!*" she sobbed, writhing to one side on the floor, reaching for the crumpled dress where it lay on the carpet. "Did you have to use—that?"

"I wanted to please you," I told her.

To my amazement, tears sprang into her eyes. "You've turned me into an animal! I could forgive your inability to perform as a man—I saw what you endured in that place!—but I c-can't forgive you this."

She held the dress before her nakedness like a timid virgin as she got to her feet. Her hands lifted the dress above her head, it slipped down over her shoulders, then to her breasts and about her hips. I could see the tears running down her cheeks, and cursed myself.

She had wanted romance, I had given her animality.

For a sexologist, I'd goofed but good.

I had as an excuse my worriment about the murder I was to commit. If I could not function as a male because of the HECATE controls on my brain, I certainly wouldn't be able to get out of assassinating Henri Planget.

I hurled the splint across the room.

Margot Metayer sniffled. She was walking toward the suite door, bending to lift her gloves and pocketbook. She said, "Keep my brassiere and my girdle. I could never wear them again, anyhow. They'd remind me of you."

The door opened and slammed shut.

I was alone with myself and my Luger.

My thoughts were chaotic. I tried to tell myself it didn't matter that I'd failed to function as a man. But I knew better. HECATE had its thumb on me, and squirm as I might, it wasn't about to let me go. I was going to have to kill a man.

"The hell with that," I growled. "I'll find a way out of this fix. Nobody turns me into a cold-blooded murderer."

Sure. All I had to do was—

I tried to empty the automatic of its bullets. I drew back the toggle assembly, tried to remove the magazine. My fingers froze on the frame.

"Come on, damn you," I whispered to the magazine. "Come out of there!" The magazine ignored me.

If I couldn't empty the gun, I'd lose it. I walked to the window, raised it and made as if to throw the Luger away.

It stuck to my fingers. More correctly, my fingers would not let go.

I put the Luger on a tabletop and sat down in a chair to stare at it. "There has to be a way out," I began in a calm, quiet manner. "I am not an assassin. I will not shoot down Henri Planget just because a couple of doctors stuck a gimmick in my head."

My nerves relaxed a little. I sat back and rested my head on the chairback. All I needed to do was think a little. Suppose I ring for room service? I'll hide the Luger under a napkin when I'm done, and the waiter will take it away with him.

If he brings it back, I'll simply deny that it's mine. I'll say I've never seen it before.

I reached for the phone to ring room service.

The club sandwich they brought me, the pot of coffee and the double Scotch on the rocks were all delicious. The napery was white and big. It would hide the automatic perfectly. I would give the waiter a big tip and meet him at the door with the tea tray.

It worked out fine—in theory.

When the time came to hide the Luger under the napkin, I couldn't do it. My hand was nerveless. It refused to transfer the gun from the table where I'd put it to the tea tray. I swore a blue streak, but even my considerable cussword vocabulary was no help.

I went to bed with visions of executioners and guillotines dancing around in my head. My only consolation was the notion that sometimes the subconscious mind will solve a problem which the conscious mind cannot, after a period of sleep.

My subconscious was on vacation. I woke up no better off than before. I lay there, staring at the ceiling, and I told myself to get cracking, because tomorrow at high noon, I was going to be forced into killing a man unless I found a way out.

"And I can't kill him. I just can't!"

I got another harebrained scheme. I would get dressed, go downstairs with my Luger in the shoulder holster, and when I saw a flic, I would yank out the gun and threaten him with it. The cop would lock me up, and Henri Planget would live to a ripe old age.

Ha! Ha!

I walked right up to a policeman, but I could no more have taken the Luger out of its holster than I could have jumped a mile into the air. When he looked at me inquiringly, I bowed politely and asked the way to the Louvre.

Scratch another idea.

Maybe if I went to some slum corner of Paris, a St. Denis tough might rob me. He would steal the Luger and my troubles would be over. So I waved down a taxi and told the driver to take me to the Quartier Latin.

I walked the dimly lighted streets of the Latin Quarter, as safe as a novice nun at Mass. Nobody even looked at me twice. As I gave up on that idea, I wondered what I would have done if somebody had tried to rob me. Maybe my controlled mind would have forced me to defend myself.

So I went back to my hotel room and brooded.

I had to think about my predicament. The idea came to me that I was able to talk about it, so why not talk to somebody on the telephone? I dialed the police station nearest the Plaza-Athénée.

When a desk sergeant answered, my tongue stuck to the roof of my mouth. I couldn't say a word. I hung up and kicked the table leg, but all that did was give me a sore toe.

I went and got the Luger, intending to put a bullet through my foot. I could not pull the trigger.

Time was running out on me.

I was a rat in a trap that could go nowhere except where the trap let me go. I collapsed across the divan where Margot Metayer had lain yesterday. I stared at the wall across the room and damned the world.

In a little while, I was fast asleep.

Maybe the sleep did my reasoning processes some good, or maybe it was my subconscious mind functioning. Whatever the cause, when I opened my eyes I had another brainstorm.

I said slowly, to test my theory, "I am supposed to kill a man today, at twelve o'clock noon, as he comes out of the Chateau Frontenac Hotel. He is a high official in the North American Treaty Organization. I am going to kill him because I cannot help myself."

I paused, grinning. No problem so far.

83

All I needed now was a tape recorder and—

I got out of bed, got dressed and went downstairs. I inquired at the desk as to the nearest store which sold tape recorders. There was such a store within easy walking distance, I was told.

I paid close to twenty thousand francs for the recorder, but it would be worth it, if it worked. I asked the clerk who sold me the recorder if he knew where I could find a spiral disc.

A spiral disc is a round piece of metal on which a black spiral is traced. It is used to hypnotize patients by doctors and psychiatrists. There is usually a small electric motor attached to it so that the disc turns slowly or swiftly. By staring at the rotating spiral, a person can be hypnotized more or less easily.

The clerk did not know where I could buy such a thing. "On second thought," he amended as he handed me my change, "There's a supply house over on the Rue de Coq Bleu."

The Rue de Coq Bleu it should be, then.

In an hour I had both my tape recorder and the spiral disc up in my room. I called room service for ham and scrambled eggs, toast and coffee. What I was about to do would proceed better if I had a full stomach. I would be sleepy with food, and fall prey more easily to the spinning disc.

I began speaking casually, turning on the tape recorder. "You are going to fall asleep. You are very tired, exhausted. Exhausted. You ache pleasantly in every muscle. You are going to fall asleep, fall asleep. . . .

"Sleep, sleep, sleep. . . .

"You are very tired. Very tired. Your eyelids are so heavy you cannot keep them open. Close your eyelids. Close your eyelids. And sleep. . . .

"Sleep. . . ."

I have hypnotized students in my sociology courses, as well as in my League For Sexual Dynamics studies. I have taken courses in the subject and I am considered an expert in the field. I have even hypnotized myself, to test my powers, as part of my sexual studies.

I talked for half an hour until I was certain that I should be in a deep hypnotic trance, were I staring into

84

the rotating spiral disc. Hypnotism is based on suggestion. If a hypnotized man is told he is eating a heavy meal, his body itself will function as if he had in truth eaten that meal. His stomach will produce the proper digestive juices, he will feel full, he may even get a few indigestion pains.

A man can be made to remember things under hypnosis, or to forget people and events, even to be insensible to pain. He can be compelled to believe he acted in certain ways—for instance, that he had taken a trip—when in fact he had acted in a completely different manner.

I did not know whether I could hypnotize myself into not shooting down Henri Planget but it was my last hope. If it failed, I was going to be a murderer.

I went on speaking into the tape recorder.

"You are going to keep your appointment outside the Chateau Frontenac Hotel. You will carry your Luger automatic with you as you perform all the acts precedent to the moment when you are to pull the trigger. You will not—I repeat, *not*—pull the trigger of the Luger. You can aim it, after you make certain no one can see you —but you will not be able to pull the trigger.

"You will come out of the hypnotic trance after Henri Planget has disappeared from sight.

"I repeat, you will act perfectly normally, as if you were going to shoot Henri Planget. You will make certain you are not observed as you take up your post. You will draw and hold and aim the Luger, if you are sure no one is looking at you. But you will not be able to pull its trigger. Your trigger finger has no strength. Your trigger finger has no strength."

I went on like that until the tape ended and the recorder clicked off. I sighed and sat back in my chair. My forehead was wet with sweat. My hands were shaking in reaction.

I rewound the tape, set it to repeat.

Then I got the little electric motor with the spiral disc on it, placing it beside the tape recorder. I plugged in the motor and rested both my hands on the buttons. I pressed at both buttons exactly the same moment.

The wheel began to revolve. So did the tape. I fastened my eyes on the slowly spinning disc. My ears would hear

85

the tape, but I must be in the hypnotic trance for my words to be effective.

I went under almost at once.

For the next hour I knew absolutely nothing. I only came to when the tape recorder clicked off. Still sleepy, I reached out and shut off the disc.

The normal hypnotic subject does not know the things he has been told in the trance. Since I was hypnotizing myself, I did know. I drew a deep breath. Would it work? Would my subconscious mind prevent me from pulling the Luger trigger? Had I tricked it sufficiently? I did not know.

I would only know when I aimed the Luger at Henri Planget and tried to kill him. If it worked, I was back in business as a Coxeman. If it did not, I was still a tool of HECATE, and an assassin.

My wristwatch informed me it was time to go. I strapped on the shoulder holster and thrust the Luger into it. I told myself glumly that even if my scheme did work, how was HECATE going to react to my failure? HECATE might even send out a radio command for me to kill myself.

I was gambling that they would not know.

HECATE would wonder *why* I had failed. HECATE would want to learn the answer to that, and so they would keep me alive, if only to tell them.

I hoped.

I dismantled the spiral disc and erased the message on the tape. I stored both these objects in my valise, which I locked. It was past eleven thirty. I would have to act fast if I was goiing to reach the Chateau Frontenac by noon, when Henri Planget was due to emerge from a conference.

I hailed a taxi at the corner and gave the driver instructions to let me off at the Rue Pierre Charron, two blocks away from the Chateau Frontenac. I was counting on the fact that the driver would never connect me with the assassination at that hotel, should it go so far, if he tied me in with a different destination.

I got out of the taxi, paid my fare with a good if not too liberal tip, and walked away. I went in the direction opposite that of the Chateau Frontenac, in case the driver should later be questioned by the flics.

Then I doubled back.

At five minutes to high noon, I was in a room overlooking the sidewalk just outside the hotel. The Luger was loose in my shoulder holster and my heart was hammering madly in my rib cage. I had signed the hotel register under an assumed name, I had paid my bill, since I had no luggage, telling the clerk I was so tired after an all night train ride that I must have sleep immediately.

My first act upon entering my room was to throw up the window and study the sidewalk. I had a good ten feet in which to put a bullet in Henri Planget's head. If I were a dedicated HECATE agent, I could have acted in no better way.

I drew back behind a drape. The Luger was in my hand. My wristwatch read twelve noon.

Where was my victim?

I held my breath. Maybe something had detained him, maybe the news of what was to happen had leaked out. I was a sitting duck here for the police if they should come to question me.

Then I saw him. Henri Planget had been a military man before he became an NATO official. His back was very straight, his head was held high. He made a perfect target, walking slowly, savoring the crisp Parisian air.

The Luger lifted, steadied.

I had him framed in my sight. I could no more have missed him than I could have fallen down. I was sweating, seeing his head just beyond my gunsight. My trigger finger curled.

Was I going to shoot?

CHAPTER FIVE

Yes!

The electrode in my skull was sending out its orders. Kill Planget! Kill Planget! It was a voice within me, powering my muscles, making me unable to refuse. My lips writhed back, I forced my mind to cancel out that call—and could not.

Inexorably my finger tightened. The Luger trigger was cold to my flesh. Cold! In an instant the gun would be spitting lead.

Below me, Henri Planget walked on.

I could not move my trigger finger! It would go only so far, and then it became a bar of rigid steel. My mind reeled with relief; at the same time my entire body shuddered at the command that other part of my brain was sending out, that could not be obeyed.

Henri Planget got into the car. The car pulled away.

The command in my brain died out. I slumped against the window frame, shaking all over, attacked by an ague of agony. I had not committed murder! My autohypnotic act had taken over my subconscious mind; it had refused to let my conscious brain obey that call to kill.

I was limp with relief. I just leaned into the wood and closed my eyes, my arm falling to my side, weighted down by the automatic.

I drew several deep breaths. It had been a near thing, a damn near thing. Now all I had to do was face HECATE and deny that I had interfered with their radio transmitter. What kind of cock-and-bull story could I concoct that they would believe? I had no idea.

It was enough for me at this moment to know I was innocent of a man's blood, that I was free—for a little while—to do what I wanted to do as a person, not as a flesh-and-blood automaton.

I lay down on the bed and tried to relax. There was really only one possibility open to me. I had to go to the Coxe Foundation office here in Paris and get them to put a new counter-transmitter into my body.

I waited four hours, then I got off the bed, left the hotel, caught a taxi at the corner and gave the driver a street address on the Rue Majory; 45 Rue Majory was where the Foundation had its Parisian headquarters behind the guise of a real estate office.

A tall man with wide shoulders and the look of a prize-fighter asked me what properties I might be interested in. I told him I was a visitor to Paris, and that my name was T.X. Coxe. Since this is the name of him who began the Thaddeus X. Coxe Foundation, the man blinked, smiled faintly, and bowed me to the rear of the agency.

His hand touched a section of the wall. An opening appeared as a large panel slid back. I stepped through into what seemed to be another office. A girl with long red hair smiled at me.

I murmured, "I need an operation. I'm working against HECATE."

She got up and walked with a pronounced back and forth movement of her rump toward a closed door. She spoke into a concealed microphone. The door slid back and the girl turned to motion me forward.

"Mademoiselle Etampes will see you now." She smiled.

To my surprise, there was a young woman behind the big oak desk toward which I advanced. In France, I suddenly remembered, there were such things as Coxewomen, so I tried to be as Continental as possible; I made a little bow and kissed the hand she extended.

"My, my. A regular cavalier," she enthused. "You must be happy about something. Care to tell me?"

I told her the entire story.

When I was done, Yvette Etampes nodded, her eyes thoughtful. "Of course, they discovered the counter-stimulator in your body and removed it. We can put another one in quite easily, but will it escape their detection?"

"How about my tooth? I have a cavity that's fairly

89

large. All we really require is a pulsometer, anything that will emit enough of a signal to disturb the radio signals to the Hecate electrode. Something simple."

She dimpled, "You make it sound so easy. Wait. Let me make a phone call to one of dental staff."

I listened as she explained what she needed and waited as she listened in turn to the voice on the other end of the line. She covered the speaker section of the phone and looked at me.

"Can do, with ease," she told me. "All that remains is to set the time and place."

"As fast as possible. I'm on my getaway route, but I do have to report back to HECATE within a reasonable time limit."

"Right now? I'll drive you there."

I nodded. She spoke a few more words, got to her feet and reached for her gloves and handbag. I was discovering that my sex restrictions were gone, because as she leaned ovsr, her blouse dipped away from her pert chest, giving me an excellent view of her white breasts and pert red nipples. My manhood became interested.

Well, *that* was a relief!

I thought about Margot Metayer and promised myself I would try to make amends to her if ever I got the chance again. I really did owe her a reward. Through her, I had found out I wasn't in control of my bodily reactions. This meant that if she hadn't tried to get me to lay her, I'd never have known I had to go through with the shooting of Henri Planget, and I'd have become an assassin.

Trailing my fellow Foundation agent down the hall, studying the jiggle of her buttocks in her tight linen dress, it was a distinct pleasure to find I was a man again, believe me. Yvette Etampes was a Coxewoman with whom I would love to become better acquainted.

Unfortunately, this was not in the stars.

She was all business as she gestured me to enter the little red Citroen parked behind the real estate agency. The fact that she showed off her shapely nyloned legs getting behind the wheel and that she drove with her skirt bunched about her full upper thighs, apparently went unnoticed by her. Not until she braked into a curbstone

90

and her red mouth twitched into a smile, did I realize she was teasing me.

"Come see me when your tooth is better," she invited.

"I most certainly will," I promised.

It was a promise I was not to keep. They had been expecting me in the dental office. A nurse whisked me past a couple of waiting patients into a small room fitted out with dental chair and drill. A man in a white uniform was waiting quietly.

He stuck his mirror in my mouth, nodding as I informed him that I had a cavity fully capable of containing a pulsometer, if it was small enough.

"We have just the thing. I'll have to prepare it, however, in case HECATE takes X-rays of your mouth. We can't have them discovering another one on you, now can we?"

I shivered at the thought. The dentist told me to stay where I was, that it would take time to embed the pulsometer in a lead casing.

I dozed for about an hour.

His touch on my arm woke me. He was quite happy, he had been able to fit a microscopic pulsometer into a tiny bit of lead. He would cover it with silver so that it seemed only a normal filling.

An hour later, I got out of the chair. It had not hurt, despite the drilling required. The dentist told me I would not notice the pulsations given off by the tiny gadget. Until I wanted to disobey the commands HECATE fed me, that is. Then I would be damn glad it was in my mouth.

He shook my hand. "Good Luck!"

I walked out onto the street. It was my duty to report to HECATE. I had to have a story to tell them. Maybe I could make it up on the drive back. I hailed a taxi, told the driver to take me to the Plaza-Athénée, where I had parked the scarlet Lamborghini Miura.

I fortified myself for the drive back to Dampierre with two martinis, a thick slice of *entrecôte,* served medium rare, a Caesar salad, and three Pernods, in the hotel dining room. I took my time. I was in no hurry to face my employers. They would not be in a nice mood.

Nor would I, I reflected. I must appear to be bitterly

91

distressed at not having carried out the task set me. My indignation must be far superior to their distrust. How could one be a good and competent secret agent, a killer, if one had not the proper tools?

Yes, this must be my approach.

I thought about it as I paid the bill, I ruminated over it as I slid into the Lamborghini Miura. I tossed it back and forth in my mind all the way along the road to Dampierre As I drove, my anger mounted.

I entered the hospital lobby like a hurricane, tossing my attache case (that held my Luger and its shoulder strap) onto a chair and shouting, "Fools! Fools! Has the world nothing but fools?"

A nurse hurried toward me, making shushing motions.

"Please, m'sieu. *S'il vous plais!* be quiet! We have sick people all about us."

"I, too, am sick, nurse! I demand to see Doctor Roger-Viollet immediately!"

She nodded, giving me an odd look, then turned her back and marched ahead of me like a sergeant-major. She took me up a flight of stairs and to a dark wooden door. She knocked.

The door opened almost immediately. Doctor Cyrano Matelot stood glowering at me. "Please to come in," he said stiffly.

I brushed past him, almost stiff-arming him out of the way. His look of surprise was grotesque. So, too, was that of Yves Roger-Viollet, sitting at his ease behind his doctorial desk.

"Fools! Imbeciles! Is this who serves HECATE?" I roared.

"We're asking ourselves that very question," snapped Matelot to one side of me. "You failed, Professor Damon. Hecate does not take kindly to failures."

I pushed my face within an inch of his own. "Is this a trick? Are you testing me, as you did in that maze? If you did—if that trip to Paris was just another of your researches as to my character—I consider myself insulted."

They were stupefied. I had no way of knowing what they expected of me, perhaps they thought to see me cringe and fawn on them, begging forgiveness. If so, my attack was not only unexpected, it was a masterstroke of Machiavellian duplicity.

Roger-Viollet muttered, "What are you talking about?"

"The Luger, man—the silly, useless automatic you gave me."

"Silly? Useless?" Matelot repeated.

I whirled on him. "Is a car any good without gasoline? Is a woman any good without a *con?* What good is a gun without bullets?"

Roger-Viollet rose to his feet, his face white. "Are you trying to excuse your failure by the falsehood that there were no bullets in the gun we gave you?"

I actually sneered, curling my lip like a villain in *East Lynne.* "Would I have failed to kill Planget if there had been bullets in the magazine?"

This was a facer. They stared at each other, then back at me. Roger-Viollet sat down slowly. He looked troubled, no longer angry.

Matelot muttered, "It could not be!"

Yves Roger-Viollet echoed, "It could not, indeed."

"Farceurs," I said angrily. "You pose and posture like wicked magicians, but your whole outfit is about as efficient as a worn-out shoe! It's a disgrace to belong to it." I added the insult supreme. "At least, when I belonged to the Coxemen, and when I was given a gun that was said to have been loaded—it was loaded. Pah!"

I turned my back on them and went to stand before an etching by Picasso. It was a good etching, it held my interest despite the fact that my spine crawled with worry-worms. Had I overacted? I hunched my shoulders as if to shrug off any thoughts of HECATE.

Roger-Viollet cleared his throat. *"M'sieu le professeur!* Your attention, please. We at HECATE do not make mistakes."

I stared at the etching as I said, "Correction! You would like to think that you make no mistakes. Actually you are all bunglers. Bunglers!"

Matelot said mildly, "It has never happened before."

I turned on them. "It will not happen again—if you want me to go on serving your moon goddess! I am not used to failure. My record until now has been one of unin-

93

terrupted success. I will not have that record ruined."

Roger-Viollet spread his hands below a pleasant smile. "We would not have it ruined either, Professor. When we heard that Henri Planget was en route to Brussels aboard a Sabena jet, we could not believe our ears. Naturally we assumed you had bungled."

"You'd blame me? Just tell me, how could I have bungled—if there'd been any bullets in that Luger? Just one was all there had to be. I had him in the sight like this."

I held out my right arm stiffly, my fingers curled about an unseen gun-stock. My eye peered down an invisible barrel. It was an impressive performance.

Cyrano Matelot honored it by muttering, "There can be no other explanation! Yves, there cannot be. He must be telling the truth."

Yves Roger-Viollet grinned wickedly. "We could ask you to take a lie detector test, but there is no need for that. You could not have disobeyed us. You *could not!* You did aim the way you so dramatically represent, Professor. You did not fire the gun. Why? You were being forced to fire it. Your body was compelled to obey that directive.

"The only sane explanation is—the gun was not loaded."

"An inexcusable mistake—on somebody's part," I growled.

"Indeed, yes," nodded Matelot. "I shall check back. Of course, whoever is guilty will lie, he or she will swear he or she loaded the magazine. We know better." He turned his head to look down at Roger-Viollet. "Ought such a one be punished for negligence?"

"Not yet. But his actions will be studied. If he makes another such error, he will be removed."

"Well? What about me?" I demanded. "I demand my record be corrected to show no mistake on my part. I refuse to take the blame for the malpractice of some underling."

Doctor Matelot moved to a mahogany liquor cabinet. He poured three glasses of Napoleon brandy in big crystal snifters. He carried them to the desk, handed one to me, one to his fellow HECATE leader, and took one himself.

"To Professor Damon—on a job well done," he smiled.

I allowed myself to be mollified. Besides, the brandy was excellent and I could not keep up my pose of injured feelings before its warmth. I sipped, I savored, I enjoyed. True Frenchmen, the doctors beamed at my obvious delight in their brandy.

"I should like another job as soon as possible," I told them, when I set down the empty glass. "I want to prove to you that I am an accomplished agent, that I can carry out orders perfectly—when stupid mistakes do not handicap me."

Roger-Viollet murmured, "We may have an assignment for you, Professor. One on which you can prove your boast of never having known a failure."

"Good," I snapped. "Let's have it."

"Oh, not so fast," laughed Matelot. "Things like this take time to plan. You take it easy for a few days. Familiarize yourself with the grounds. Get to know your fellow HECATE-workers."

It was good advice, I told myself. If I were ever to find a way to topple HECATE, I had to know its layout, its alarm systems, its secret traps and obstacles. This was as good a time as any to learn what I might expect if ever I got the chance to lead an attack on this stronghold.

I made my adieus. I found a blonde nurse down the hall and asked her to show me to my room. She giggled and stepped along beside me, chattering away, casually telling me she knew Claudette Marly, and that Claudette had mentioned me. It was a hint I could not overlook without making an enemy.

One of my duties was to get to know my fellow HECATE-workers, Doctor Matelot had said, so I made myself as charming as possible. When we stood aside to let three doctors pass, I urged my loins into the nurse's soft buttocks. My manhood reacted as I have trained it to do. I heard her gasp and felt her sideways motion with the underside of a thigh as she took a rough kind of measurement. She gasped.

I whispered into her pink ear, "You're almost too exciting."

After that it was apple pie with ice cream. She put herself out like a carpet, at my complete disposal. I went from cellar to attic space in the hospital, I met doctors and nurses and interns. The hospital itself is run quite legally and aboveboard, except for the operations involving the implanting of the radio stimulators. Those took place in the new wing of the second floor.

During those moments when we were alone, I found opportunities to draw the blonde nurse, whose name was Jeannette Lons, into empty rooms, to kiss her pouting lips with darting tongue and assess the curves of her body with wandering hands. I found out she wore a brassiere to hold in her C-cup shapes and a garterbelt to hold up her nylon stockings.

"We could lock the door of an unused room," she challenged.

"Later, pussycat. I want to see the other unit."

The back of her hand brushed my front. "You'll lose it. I don't want that to happen."

"It won't. You'll find that abstinence, for a brief period, will make the hard grow fonder."

"Oooh," she half-giggled, "you made a funny."

We went all over HECATE territory, through the maze, which I discovered was quite a layout, with machinery hidden inside the partitioned walls that could cause all kinds of accidents and oddments to happen in the maze rooms themselves. Those walls could blaze with blinding light, with heat, they could form psychedelic patterns of color combinations that could make a man so dizzy he would fall down. They could even grow frigid, turning the maze rooms into refrigerators. HECATE must have spent a fortune on this labyrinth.

The heart of this murder maze was up above, in a combination control and observation booth. Here were the glittering metallic panels fitted with the levers, dials, studs and buttons that controlled and governed the actions of the HECATE agents, sending out their radio directions to the control buttons inset in their heads. It was a large room, there were chairs for any onlookers invited to witness the testing of a candidate. Like diplomats' wives, especially one named Margot Metayer.

"Sometimes a man is executed in the maze," Jeannette murmured. "When an agent fails his assignments too often, or needs a lesson in discipline, he's put in here.

96

Nobody fails HECATE very often. Only one man was executed. He was roasted to death. He took two days to die, they did it so skillfully. He was screaming in pain all that time. We were all forced to watch.

She shuddered. "I'll never forget it. Never!"

I thought about what she had said. If I did not fulfill my next assignment, they might do that to me. It was not a nice thought. I felt like puking.

To take my mind off unpleasantness, I ran my palm down the blonde nurse's back to her behind. I toyed with her cheeks for a few minutes, until she was wriggling her thighs together.

"I guess I've seen it all," I murmured, kissing her soft throat. "Except for the way in or out. The private way, the HECATE way."

Her eyes got misty as she turned her head so my lips could move down into the vee of her white, starched uniform. "There isn't any. Or if there is, they don't tell us nurses. The front gateway is the only way I know."

She was telling the truth, I was positive. There had to be a private way in or out. But maybe they didn't tell the nurses.

She breathed, "However, I myself possess a private way."

"I am going to find that out for myself, my little pussycat."

She turned, clamped an arm about me and spread her lips over mine. For a moment we wedged together, grinding bellies. There was a heat in her dying to explode, as there was in me, I found, responding to her savagery. My fingers clamped in her soft buttocks, I lifted her up by her behind and ground her against me.

She sobbed and whimpered; she threw back her head and stared blindly at the ceiling, gasping. This one was a volcano rumbling to overflow, deep inside. In a moment, her juices would be spewing forth as Vesuvius erupted with its lavas.

I told myself it would be cruelty to wait. If I had to cement a friendship, if I must get to know my fellow worker, there was no time like the present. Besides, if Jeannette Lons were to go for me and my love-making, I would have made an ally inside the HECATE curtain.

97

I caught her tongue between my teeth. I bent down, drawing her after me, still gripping her tongue. My hands went to her stockinged thighs under her short skirt. As I drew my palms along her stockinged thighs up to bare flesh, my wrists raised her skirt.

My fingers held her nude buttocks.

My knees were bent in a crouching position. "Step on my knees," I whispered, letting go her tongue. I felt her weight add itself to my own. My leg muscles bulged.

"Squat!" I rasped, hastily baring my manhood.

She squatted, sliding herself onto me.

This was not a posture to recommend for general use. But my body was physically fit, I was in perfect condition for fight or frolic, so it added piquancy to a situation that had threatened to get sloppy. My hands held her behind, supporting her weight, her own legs against mine gave further support. This way, should there be an interruption, all Jeannette had to do was dismount and her skirt would fall into place. Now if only I had a chair under me.

She was twisting her hips in a rotary motion, making little circles. Her breath was a bellows in the air, thick and heavy. Slowly, so as not to unbalance her, I backed up, with my blonde nurse riding me.

"I've never—tried anything like—" she sobbed.

"I'm an expert in this sort of thing," I reminded her. "I know ways and means from all over the world, which I teach my L.S.D. pupils."

She gasped, squirming. "America! What a land! Do they—really—teach this in—in your country?"

I felt a chair with the backs of my straining legs. I lowered myself, at the same time easing her shoes off my lower thighs. Her heels had been digging into me, but the pain had been a kind of algolagnic thing, where it became almost pleasure. Now straddling my thighs, her feet were on the floor and she could raise and lower herself like an erotic elevator.

She went on and on, sobbing and moaning, tightening herself about me, hips jerking spasmodically from time to time. Once her eyes opened to stare blindly at me, and I thought I could detect tears of sheer delight behind her lashes.

98

I guess we were just lucky. Nobody walked into the control room while we were there, and my watch said we had been at it for over an hour. In that time, Jeannette Lons became my sexual slave. I brought her to more than a dozen orgasms. She was so limp when she was done that she lay against me, incapable of moving.

I had to lift her off, help her stand.

"Claudette didn't know the half of it," she whispered. "You're a god, Professor. A human Priapus. But I guess a lot of women have told you that."

"You're just flattering me," I said, grinning, "but I love it. Here, let me help you pull your uniform down—there."

"No, I mean it. I'd do anything for you. If you're going to be here long, why don't you come live with me?"

She sighed, smiling faintly as if with post-coital sadness. "I guess you're laughing at me. You must get a lot of offers like that."

"You have an apartment near here? I thought everybody stayed here. I didn't know the personnel had outside living quarters."

"Most everybody does. A few live here most of the time, like Doctors Roger-Viollet and Matelot, and some of the guards who rotate around-the-clock duties. They're only in the maze compound, though. The hospital itself is run quite normally."

I was learning things. I didn't know how I could take advantage of the knowledge, or whether I ever would, but I stored the facts away in my head as a squirrel stores nuts in autumn.

"I suppose you think this is a ridiculous question, but if I wanted to sneak in without being noticed—for instance, suppose you and I were out on a date and I had to drop you off at your place—let's say I was on call here at headquarters and I didn't want anybody to know I'd been goofing off—when could I best slip in unobserved?"

She giggled. "Oh, between one and two in the morning. The guards change at one. By the time they make their rounds and take up their positions, it's two. If you knew how they make those rounds, you could anticipate them and be where they were sure not to be."

I hugged her. "You've got to tell me about all that,

99

Jeannette. We may forget that sort of thing while we're out dancing—"

"I should hope so!" she exclaimed.

"—so it's better to know beforehand."

She glanced at her wristwatch. "I'm off duty in half an hour. Why don't you go rest in your room? Then we can go some place and talk."

"Just talk?"

She patted my frontal bulge, eyebrows raising. "Oh? What's this? You still want more?"

"I'm just a hungry lover." I laughed.

"May you always have a hearty appetite!" she giggled, squeezing, groping. Her eyes turned thoughtful. "Really, I mean it. There's no law says we can't go dancing tonight. I know a little place. Not expensive."

"It's a date. I'll change my clothes and wait in my room." I drew her to me for a last kiss. "You're my girlfriend, remember. Stay away from those guards."

Her laughter rang out. "Those *milksops!* Pah! The most manly of them is too effeminate for me." Her wise eyes taunted me. "It is what makes one so easy to tumble, working here. There are so many nurses and so few real men. You understand?"

I kissed the corners of her mouth. *"Je comprends."*

I went down to my room after parting company with my pretty blonde nurse. I lay down on the bed to think, not to sleep. I was no nearer a solution of my assignment—the destruction of HECATE—than I was when I set foot on French soil. If it had an Achilles' heel, I failed to see it. I'd damn near murdered a man, I'd failed a woman in the love act, I'd gotten a radio stimulator put into my skull. That was it, the whole bit.

Well, I had made a friend of Jeannette Lons. I had thought my way out of the bag with Henri Planget. I was a more-or-less trusted member of HECATE. Maybe this was something. I could be dead right now.

I had to lay the groundwork for my final Armageddon, here in Dampierre. I had begun by getting my blonde nurse to show me all around the hospital and HECATE headquarters. But all alone, I'd never be able to do the destruct bit.

I needed help.

Jeannette Lons might be that help, she might not.

At any rate, I would try to swing her over to my side and fasten her there with some erotic epoxy, if that was what was needed. It might not be; I might just have caught her in a weak moment.

So when she poked her head in the door, dressed in a simple peasant blouse and skirt—she was off-duty, I remembered—I caught her cheeks in my palms and drew her gently into my room for a tender kiss. Our lips merged, I let my mouth tell her mouth that I loved her very much. Her eyes were like stars when I drew away.

She understood I didn't think of her as just a body. There was also what was inside the body, the soul, the ka, the essence, which attracted me. Even her mind. It all played a part in the whole Jeannette Lons.

"Tell me what you are," I breathed into her parted lips. I smiled at her look of surprise. "You eat food, you like certain foods. I want to know them. I want to know what games you played as a child. What it is that frightens you, what you like or dislike. Everything. Tell me everything."

She put her arms about my neck and hugged me. "It will take forever, you goose. You nice goose. I think you are trying to make me fall in love with you. Are you?"

I kissed the tip of her nose. "Who can tell?"

It took four days, actually.

We went to the flea market in Dampierre, we bought silly things like a cracked vase with flowers on it (she liked roses, and there were big red Scarlet Knights on the vase), a small toy soldier made by Mignot (she had been a tomboy as a child, playing with her brothers' lead *soldats*), and a book of poetry all about love. We ate escargots at a sidewalk table and drank tart red wine while we took turns reading the poems out loud. She wept a little at one of the quatrains, saying she had heard it as a child.

In the red Lamborghini Miura, we drove to the chateau for which Dampierre is famous and walked through its park, hand in hand. She stopped to sniff the flowers and flirted with me as if we were, in truth, the lovers we pretended to be. Perhaps we were. As I traveled on my Coxeman assignments about the world I have discovered one fundamental truth, that a man or a woman may fall in

101

love over and over again. It is a philosophy that has protected me against a lot of heartaches.

We motored to Chartres and visited the cathedral. We made a trip to Versailles and strolled through the Parc de Trianon and along the walks of the Great Canal. The sunlight on her cheeks, the wind in her blonde hair, the laughter from her red lips, built a song in my heart.

I stayed overnight in her little room some blocks from the hospital. We were like husband and wife, newlyweds. We made love tenderly, we explored the love-in likes and dislikes of each other. Sometimes in the very early morning, I could hear her sigh as she lay naked beside me under the covers.

Our little idyll was going to end some day soon. She knew it, I knew it, we both pretended we did not. When she would sigh, I would lean over and kiss her bare shoulder, or perhaps the upper swell of a breast. She would smile weakly, then laugh and tousle my hair with her gentle hand.

Once I said, "Why don't you get a job somewhere else?" I was thinking of the coming destruction of HECATE, if I did my job as I should. I could not think of her being caught in the holocaust.

"Where would I work?" she asked, turning from the tiny stove where she was making a cheese fondue while I was opening a wine bottle.

"Oh, I don't know. Somewhere. Anywhere but for HECATE. I consider it dangerous work for a girl."

"I'm only a nurse. Nothing criminal about that." She shrugged with the nonchalance of the young. "They pay better wages than I could get anywhere else. To me, that is reason enough."

I discontinued that sort of talk for fear she might become suspicious. I had not put aside the thought that Jeannette Lons might be a spy sicced on me by Doctor Roger-Viollet. If she were, I felt convinced, she was a better actress than any woman on the stage or in the movies.

One morning I was summoned to headquarters.

Doctor Matelot was sitting behind the desk, examining the file. He nodded at my entrance, invited me to sit down.

"*Bon jour,* Professor. You are in luck. A case has

102

come up where we think you might be the man for the job."

"Good," I exclaimed, wondering what was good about it. I was enjoying my visit to the Elysian Fields with Jeannette Lons, and I didn't want it to end.

His eyes regarded me calmly. "You may not think it is so good when you hear what it is. You see, we of HECATE have made certain contacts in the political and military world beyond our gates. We have made friends, we have made enemies. There are also those who try to straddle the fence. They are neither for us nor against us.

"We have a fourth category, those who have been our friends but who have now turned against us. These we must lure back to the fold—or exterminate. Such a one is General René Bree."

"Ah! I am to kill the general."

Matelot smiled, "Oh, no. You are to kill his wife."

He was right. I did not think it was good at all.

CHAPTER SIX

I kept my poker face. I even smiled.

"I see," I murmured. "First the wife, then the general. It is a military technique of some sort."

"It's nothing of the kind," Matelot snapped. "The general has been warned several times. He has chosen to ignore our warnings. The death of his wife will be the act that will bring him over to our side."

I shook my head. "I don't see why you don't control him the way you control other people."

"Unfortunately he is one person we have not been able to implant. Twice we have tried, twice he has escaped an injury which would necessitate his going into a hospital. I believe, myself, that he is suspicious of us. If it were up to me, I would have him killed."

"But if—that is, when I kill his wife, won't he blab to the authorities about this HECATE setup?"

"While he has not been implanted with a radio stimulator, his secretary—who is also his mistress—has been. She serves us. She will notify us if he has any such ideas. So far, he has been detached from the entire situation. Besides his wife, he has two daughters he loves. Understand?"

"Hmmm. His wife he does not love? He tolerates her?"

"She controls the family fortunes. The money is in her name. If she were to die, the general would be a very rich man. In a way, then, HECATE is doing him a favor."

"Will he understand and appreciate that favor?"

"He will understand it, *oui*. Whether he appreciates it is another matter. If he does not appreciate it, he will infer that as the mother died, so can either or both of his daughters. He is not a stupid man, the general."

"And he loves his daughters."

104

Maletot inclined his head. "He will not be happy to see either of them dead, I can assure you of that. And he will want very much to enjoy the vast fortune he will come into when his wife dies. He will not be able to do that if he does not come over to HECATE. And soon."

It was arm-twisting on a cold-blooded level.

I faked admiration at the scheme. "He can't fail to become one of our allies. I certainly contratulate you on you cleverness. It gives me a good feeling to know I'm part of such an organization. Provided," I added slyly, "the underlings do what they're supposed to, like load guns that are to kill people."

Maletot said coldly, "The gun will be loaded this time, never fear. I am going to do it myself."

Our interview was not over. Matelot glanced down at the open file before him. He cleared his throat.

"Madame Sabine Bree is to be in Copenhagen this evening. Her husband is on his way to Moscow for a conference with the military heads of the Soviet Union. When he goes on such extended visits to a foreign country, his wife also takes herself off on holiday."

He permitted himself a smile. "She is what we French call a *garçonniere,* the woman free with men, a nymphomaniac. She would have killed the general long ago, if she had concerned herself with him alone. Sometimes I think he goes off on these missions to give her a chance to get rid of her *joie de vivre.* She does, and with a vengeance, anywhere she travels. She has a way of finding sympathetic souls who are only too happy to indulge her and their own passions. But this you will discover for yourself.

"Naturally, we don't expect you to walk in with your loaded Luger and shoot her down dead. *Mais non!* We enjoy finesse in this as in any other facet of life. You are to be permitted your own method of assassination."

"As I was with Henri Planget?"

He flushed. "I begin to think that whole affair was a mistake, from its inception. No, no. You are on your own in this affair. There is no hurry. Madame Bree is not going anywhere in her Copenhagen retreat, except perhaps from one bed to another. You will pick and choose your own time.

"However, you will be watched. We shall have a girl spy on hand to keep her eyes on you, to make sure you do what you're told."

"When do I leave?" I asked.

"Tomorrow morning from the Orly Airport. Your tickets will be furnished you at the desk. *Adieu*, Professor."

I stood up, I made a little bow.

Then I went to find Jeannette Lons.

She made a face when I told her the news. I tried to console her by telling her we would have the night together, but she shook her head.

"It cannot be. I have been transferred to the night shift. You will have to sleep alone." Her lips quivered into a smile as she added, "I hope?"

I kissed her cheek as if it were a promise.

Next day at this same time I was sitting in a window seat staring down at the French countryside. The big S.A.S. plane was over wine country, the vineyards of which made a soft carpet of green through an early morning haze. I lay back and thought about Denmark, Copenhagen and Madame Bree.

Most Americans think about Denmark, if they think about it at all, as being the home of the Vikings who came and conquered England, first under Sweyn Forkbeard, secondly and more permanently, under Canute the Great. Few know that as late as the early nineteenth century, Denmark held Norway as one of its possessions. Or that during the Napoleonic Wars, suffering defeat at the hands of England—after England had bombarded Copenhagen for three days while peace existed between the two countries—she lost Norway and other rich territories.

Denmark made a remarkable comeback. From the near-bottom despair of 1814 by hard work and determination, Denmark rose again to be among the world powers, in a commercial sense. Today, its bacons, hams, cabbages and carrots form part of its biggest industry, which is the production of food. One hundred thousand tons of Danish butter finds its way into the world market annually.

An infant linen industry stands close beside the much older business of making boats. The Dane is born with the salt sea in his nostrils; it is no wonder then that it enters into his blood. The Danish fishing fleet, that numbers more than twenty-two thousand ships, brings in great catches of cod, haddock, lobster and other delicacies from the North Sea, the Baltic, the Skagerrak and Kattegat.

We circled over Kastrup Airport. I caught a glimpse of the harbor with its little bronze mermaid, and the line of parks that stand where, in medieval days, the moat had been. I looked forward to my stay in Copenhagen; I'd never been in this city, which has become the most important seaport in the Scandinavian countries and is fast getting a reputation as a swinging city to rival that of London.

Of course, I had no idea as to how I was to avoid killing Sabine Bree, or how to escape getting killed myself by the HECATE agent keeping an eye on me. I would play that by ear. I have found that some of my best ideas swing in out of left field when I'm in a jam. Like with the autohypnotism by which I'd managed to let Henri Planget live.

I recovered my luggage from the baggage section of the Scandinavian Airlines System, passed through Customs without incident, and managed to flag down a taxi. I had reservations at the Kongen af Denmark Hotel by the Homens Canal. Since the Danes enjoy food, sex and song just as much as I do, I was not worried about a thing.

All I had to do was contact *madame le general.*

Meanwhile and until then I was going to have fun. After settling my luggage in my hotel room, I took off on a walking tour of Copenhagen. I dined at the Stadil, a kind of chop house where the food just about melts in your mouth. Then I strolled on toward the Tivoli Gardens, not far away.

The Tivoli Gardens threw open its gates in the summer of 1843, on the site of a great battle between the Danes and the Swedes. Today the only fighting that goes on there is an occasional elbow in the ribs as people move toward where the action is. Tivoli boasts a small lake and a veritable maze of gorgeous gardens. There is a theater, a large concert hall, and outdoor amusements that draw people here during the months of July, August and September.

The world calls Copenhagen the Paris of the North, and

a good bit of this reputation has been earned by these Tivoli Gardens. Under the shadow of the towering City Hall spire, its dance halls, restaurants and carousels attract four and a half million people annually. At night, its glittering lights form part of a fairyland that would have delighted Denmark's native son, Hans Christian Andersen.

I stopped for a Tuborg beer and watched the girls go by. They were slimly curved, attractive blondes with their golden tresses falling about their shoulders, pert brunettes, ditto, and several voluptuous creatures with glossy black hair and provocatively moving bodies. Unfortunately from my point of view, each girl was accompanied by a husky male on whose arm she leaned. Oh, well! I could look like the cat at the queen in the nursery story.

I got tired of just looking, after a time, but I was too tired to get me a pick-up date. I promised myself another night or two at the gardens, and headed for a taxi stand.

The first thing I did in my line of work next day was rent myself a Volvo. Madame Bree was living in a rented villa not far from the Elsinore beach, about thirty miles north of Copenhagan. I needed wheels to make the trip.

I slipped swim trunks on under slacks. I pulled a thickly woven sweater over my bare chest, shoved my feet into sandals, and set off. The Volvo handled sweetly, I had a picnic hamper of sandwiches prepared by the hotel cook; it was as if I were on vacation.

The Elsinore sands are almost pure white. Three miles away, across The Sound, lies Sweden. Beach attire is very informal. I simply spread a blanket, slipped out of my slacks and sweater, and I was all set for a swim.

The girls on the beach wear bikinis that show off their marvelous figures. They lie on beach towels to sun themselves and if they attract male eyes—as they know very well they do—they turn not a hair. They expect admiration as their due.

There was a brunette I might have struck up a conversation with, had I not been on duty, so to speak. With a last regretful glance at the plump tanned behind revealed by her bikini drawers, I waded out into the water.

I swam toward the Bree villa.

I had no idea of what to expect. The actuality was something out of this world. I found myself goggling at a white stucco building that occupied several levels, with a railed patio before each level, and a flight of stone steps leading to the beach. Three girls were sunning their soft flesh on that strip of white sand as I side-stroked past. As far as I could make out from across fifty yards of water, they were stark naked.

As if she had caught my thoughts, one of the girls turned over and sat up. She was bare-breasted to the sun, and when she lifted her long black hair out of her eyes, I could see the swing and bobble of those heavy orbs.

I guess she saw me then, because she got to her feet, never taking her eyes from my head as it slid through the water. There was a little black triangle at her loins that might have been a g-string or pubic hair. She started walking toward the water.

I slowed my swim pace. She came straight out toward me in a fast crawl. I stopped swimming to tread water.

In a matter of seconds, she was five feet away, kicking slowly to maintain her head above water. She said something in Danish and I hadn't the faintest notion of what she was talking about.

So I said, "Hello. Fancy meeting you here."

Her laughter was a key to unlock strangeness. She told me what she had said, in English this time, and I agreed with her that I would, indeed, like fun. Of any kind.

"I went to Tivoli yesterday, but it isn't any good without a friend along. A friend like you."

"Poooh! There are a thousand unescorted girls in the gardens. I know, I have been one of them from time to time. A nice American, unmarried—you are unmarried aren't you?—ought to have himself a ball!"

"I really wasn't trying," I admitted.

"Come ashore. I want you to meet Hannie and Kaija. Me, I'm Agnete Stralsund. You'll like them. They're secretaries during the week but over weekends they become fairy princesses like me."

"You're fairy princesses all right—if you live there." I nodded at the many-tiered villa.

"Oh, that belongs to Sabine. That is, Sabine Bree. She comes here every year with some friends of hers, all married women out for kicks. She hires the villa each time. It is quite lonely here so close to the beach, there is nobody

109

to bother us if we want to go swimming without clothes."

We had been swimming toward shore while we had been talking. There was sand underfoot now, so we walked the rest of the way. The sun was hot on our backs, it reflected off the water, which was quite clear, so I could see that the black badge below the gently mounded belly of my companion was quite natural.

She said amusedly, catching my downward glance, "As you can see for yourself. No one disturbs our little pleasures, since we disturb no one by them."

"How does one get invited to be a part of such pleasures? I had a good plane trip from Paris, and a fine sleep last night. I'm in a very healthy condition."

She gave a full laugh. "Good! We can add you to the list of candidates."

"Candidates?"

"The lady of the villa arrived only yesterday. We girls know her from other years when she has come here for a month, on what she calls her vice vacation. Nobody knows her in Denmark, though she is quite well known in Paris.

"You mentioned that you flew from Paris. Perhaps you know General Bree? This is his wife."

"I've heard of him naturally," I admitted guardedly.

"Well, since she isn't well known here, and since nobody cares one way or another what she does with her time here, she amuses herself by having contests. Sex contests."

"Ah," I breathed, understanding now why Roger-Viollet and Matelot had picked me for this job.

"She rewards the winner of the contest with a week here at her villa. The sky's the limit. If the winner wants some special treat—gastronomic or genital, it makes no difference—he is afforded what he asks for."

"And you girls supply the young men who are the contestants. A sort of labor of love. I assume she pays you well for your troubles?"

"Very well. The girl who comes up with the winner gets a nice bonus. I have never come up with a winner yet. Kaija has provided three winners. Hannie has come up with two."

"Maybe this is your lucky day," I grinned.

She was quite serious. "I hope so. I am in need of

110

money right now. The five thousand kroner that would be my prize would pay some debts and leave me a little over."

"I'll do my best," I promised.

The sound of our voices had alerted Hannie and Kaija. They turned over and sat up. Their bodies were perfectly tanned and their skin looked as richly smooth as *café au lait*. Their eyes studied my nearly naked body with the efficiency of beauty contest judges. I guess I looked all right to them, because they gave me dazzling smiles.

"He's mine," said Agnete warningly.

The two girls moved apart, offering me part of their blanket, but I felt I owed it to Agnete to sit down beside her. Hannie and Kaija made little frowns with their red lips, but Agnete looked pleased.

Kaija said, "I feel so underdressed alongside your man, Agente. Why don't you tell him to get comfortable?"

I grinned, "I'm feeling quite healthy at the moment. I might embarrass you by my reaction to so much loveliness."

"Embarrass us," smiled Hannie.

I glanced at Agnete, who shook her black head. "It would not be fair to him. He must remain strong for the contest."

"When is this contest?" I asked, visualizing a long period of unrelieved abstinence.

The girls giggled. Hannie said, "Tomorrow night. It begins at six in the evening and lasts—well, as long as it can."

Kaija added, "We are all working girls, we have to be in our offices next morning. Except Agnete, that is. She is on vacation."

I smiled at Agnete, saying, "Marvelous. So am I. We can do things together. You can show me the sights around town while I'm here. If that's all right with everybody? I don't want to be accused of stealing you away from anyone."

"It will give Agnete the opportunity of making sure you remain chaste until tomorrow," pointed out Kaija sweetly.

I was thinking that since Agnete Stralsund was on vacation, it might mean that she was taking time off to do her job as a HECATE spy. She might be the one who was to kill me if I didn't kill Madame Bree. Looking at her now,

111

in her warm nakedness, I could not believe it.

"Why not drive back to Copenhagen with me?" I invited. "We could eat somewhere, go to the Tivoli Gardens, perhaps dance at some discotheque you know."

"First I must introduce you to Madame Bree. She has to pass on your acceptibility as a contestant."

Since she probably would want to make love with the winner, it might be a good idea. I was a little curious as to what my intended victim looked like, anyhow.

We chatted for a while, then Agnete said, "I'm hungry. Come along, Rod. It's time for lunch. Sabine will be awake by this time."

It was close to one o'clock in the afternoon. "She certainly takes good care of herself," I commented.

"She is a very beautiful woman," murmured Hannie. "If sleeping makes her so glamorous, maybe I should spend more time between the sheets."

"How could you, darling?" wondered Kaija cattily.

Hannie sniffed and tossed her brunette locks. "I meant sleeping," she snapped.

Agnete reached for two bits of cloth that made up a Riviera bikini. She turned her tanned back to me as she fitted the demi-cups to her abundant breasts. I snapped the backstrap. Then she got to her feet and slipped one foot after the other between the thin spaghetti straps of the pantie portion of her suit, then wriggled it up about her creamy hips.

"He likes you, Agnete," giggled Hannie.

My bulging manhood was the target of six female eyes.

"He likes you very much," contributed Kaija.

Agnete studied me like a connoisseur, then nodded delightedly. "Maybe I will be the winner after all," she announced proudly.

I followed her long, tanned legs and switching rump up the stone steps to the first level. Sliding glass doors opened from the patio onto a stone-flagged bar room and kitchen. It was furnished in lavish taste. Its metal cabinets were tinted a light bronze, its sink matched the bronze enamel, and its bar was made of mahogany. Agnete assured me it had designed by none other than Jacobsen himself.

"I myself shall prepare your sandwich," Agnete announced.

Denmark prides itself on its open-faced sandwiches. There is a competition every year as to who can make the tallest, yet still have it within mouth-reach of the average face. Agnete set to work with pumpernickel, sliced cold cuts, pâté and fish, and thinly cut lengths of Danish cheese. She sprinkled chopped truffles across its top.

"You should have an egg too, and a glass of milk," she murmured, studying her creation.

"Aphrodisia in three dimensions," I said.

Her smile showed her even white teeth. "Of course! I am going to train you like they do a race horse. You will be in good condition when I am through."

"Could I maybe have a beer?"

She studied my lean middle, the ridges of muscles across my torso, then giggled, "All right. But just one!"

There were iced beer mugs in the refrigerator. She filled one with beer and put it on the eating counter next to the sandwich. Then she leaned her elbows on the other side and watched me eat with fond affection. I felt like a prize-fighter at the training table. The fact that her position afforded me an almost perfect view of her mammaries in the cloth cups which were far too small to hold them may have added to my appetite. She dimpled when she saw where I stared, but she did not change position.

"My bosom will stimulate your libido," she murmured.

When I was done, she came around the counter, took me by the hand and led me to the stairs. She informed me that I must meet Sabine, that she would leave me alone with her while she went back to eat her own sandwich.

The second floor contained a big living room, one wall of which was gray stone that held a huge fireplace. There were modern chairs and divans scattered all about on top of two big Persian carpets. It murmured tastefully of money.

We bypassed all this magnificence to ascend to the third level, where the bedrooms were. Outside a wide pink door Agnete paused to knock. A soft voice invited her to enter.

My first view of Sabine Bree was a stimulating one. She was wearing a thin black negligee under which she was absolutely nude. I hesitated at the door, despite the hand with which Agnete was urging me on. The negligee hung open from her throat to her dimpled knees.

113

Madame Bree smiled genially. "And who is this?" she asked in French.

"An admirer," I smiled, and bowed.

Her gray eyes glinted with amusement. She might be on vacation, but her Gallic soul appreciated the niceties of the male-female relationship. Sabine Bree was a blonde, one of those French types who have the barbarian blood of long-dead Gauls in their bodies, although here and there one might espy a gray thread or two. She was youthfully slim, mature at her heavy breasts and rounded hips, and her thighs were somewhat plumper than those of a fashion model.

She was all woman and she roused my interest. As I came closer in response to her words and the elbow with which Agnete touched me, I saw tiny crowsfeet at her eye-corners and discovered that the eyes themselves were very wise.

"I suppose you're one of the contestants?" she smiled.

"Mine," said Agnete hurriedly.

"Ah, yes. Dear Agnete. Always an entrant but never a winner. Let's hope this one will be different."

"I'll do my best," I murmured.

"Sit down, please. You will not mind if I dress?"

"It will be my pleasure," I admitted.

"But it must not be too pleasurable," Sabine Bree laughed with a sidewise glance at Agnete. "We must not interfere with the good care Agnete is taking of you."

Agnete left us then, patting my right shoulder as if to give me encouragement during my interrogation. Madame Bree observed the gesture with laughter sparkling in her gray eyes. "Agnete does not trust me," she informed me. "She knows I am a man-eater."

"To be eaten by you would be an experience to make any man proud," I told her as the door closed behind Agnete.

"Perhaps it shall come to that, m'sieu. I did not catch your name. Agnete is sometimes forgetful."

I bowed a second time. "Professor Damon, madame. Rod to my friends, among whom I hope to number you."

"*Professeur?* Of what, please?"

She was opening the negligee as she spoke, so that it made a contrast to the white flesh of her mature body. She

114

was in her early forties—a pampered, massage-parlor-and-beauty-shoppe forties, which means she looked about thirty—with heavy breasts boasting large brown nipples, a deeply indented navel, and a blonde privacy that had been recently barbered. She was an exciting woman with an aura of sexuality about her that touched a man where he lived.

She stood there with the black gossamer behind her, held by her back-thrown arms. Her gray eyes challenged me.

"Of sociology," I answered. "And as a sideline, I am also the founder and chief teacher for the League of Sexual Dynamics."

Interest blazed in her stare. "Explain this sexual dynamics, *s'il vous plait*. Is it some kind of cult?"

"Oh, no. I teach the techniques of sex and its benefits to the human body. I tell my pupils that many of our modern ills are caused by the fact that our animal natures are restricted by the modes and manners of a civilization that too often regards sex mystiques as something dirty and degrading. I seek to give them the Eastern approach, that sexual coition and its many byways are an art to be learned and studied all the life long."

"You joke with me," she pouted.

"On the contrary, it is quite true. Your Agnete is more fortunate than she knows. I think it is quite likely I shall emerge the winner in your love-in contest."

"You know many ways to make love?" she asked.

"So many, from so many lands, they sometimes get mixed up in my head. The *purshayet* position mentioned by the erotologists of India, as an instance, sometimes becomes the *nik el kohoul* of the Arabs—an entirely different love posture, as you no doubt know."

Her eyes flickered. She glanced at the brief swimsuit I wore, that did little to hide the fact that I was an amply endowed, eager young man. Madame Bree sighed and let the negligee fall to the floor behind her. She turned and showed me her body in profile, then faced away from me and walked toward the door of her dressing closet.

Her buttocks shook very gently above handsome legs.

"The oval inlet type of pelvis," I murmured, "a typically

115

European hip structure. Pelvises with round or circular inlets can be found in the South Sea islands, in Malaysia, among certain aborigine tribes. Interesting, isn't it?"

She turned at the door, looking at me as she might look at a particularly attractive painting she was considering for her collection. "If your performance can match your knowledge, *m'sieu le professeur*—you will make me a very happy woman."

It was a question, the way she said it. I bowed the third time. "I am so confident of that, madame, I am willing to make a little wager."

Her plucked eyebrows lifted. "What sum do you want to bet?"

My hand made a contemptuous gesture. "Money, pah! I am a sensualist, madame. I am more interested in the—ah, shall I say, the intangibles of life rather than in the tangibles. If I win the contest and if the prize is to be a week in your company at the villa—permit me to call the shots, so to speak, on how we shall live that week."

"I do that," she murmured thoughtfully. "Yet if you prove interesting enough during the competition, I am willing to agree to give you two days off out of the seven. Is it enough?"

It was actually more than I'd hoped for. I needed those two days to dictate situations because I hoped in that time to learn which of the pretty girls decorating the villa was my fellow HECATE agent. I thought I knew a way to find that out. All I asked was a chance to try it.

"It will be perfect," I said.

"Now," she announced, "you may zip me up the back."

She reached into her closet and brought but one of those black lastex and red lace garments that are called a Merry Widow. It would cinch in her middle and the tiny half-circles at the top would permit the breasts to hang free. Dangling garters would allow her to secure her stockings.

Mme. Bree fitted her nudity into the garment and turned her back to me. The Merry Widow gaped from the middle of her bare back to the cleavage of her buttocks.

I stepped close. My fingers gripped the flaps of the corset. "A woman was designed by *le bon Dieu* to know the admiration of a male—everywhere," I murmured, and

116

bent to run my lips from the nape of her neck to the sacral dimples just above her buttocks.

She shivered as I let my kisses wander downward to her soft behind. Was it my imagination, or was that a moan in her throat? I rose upward and began hooking the corset to her body.

"If I did not want poor Agnete to win the contest, I would myself test out your fitness," she hissed softly.

"You would not tire me, madame," I stated boldly, "though I must admit you would prove very titillating."

She swung around and eyed me carefully. "You are a braggart, *m'sieu le professur.* I hope for your sake you do not boast very often."

"And not now. Especially not now."

Her eyes brooded at me. Above the cup rims, her soft white breastflesh quivered and her dark red nipples were long and rigid. In the black corselet, with her legs bare from her hips downward, the dangling garterstraps like fingers trembling there, she made an erotic picture. A picture that tempted me mightily.

I refused temptation and made my fourth bow.

Then I turned and walked to the door. An instant before I could touch its knob, the door opened. Madame Margot Metayer stood there, gaping at me.

CHAPTER SEVEN

She was even more surprised than I.

"You! Here?" she gasped.

Over my shoulder, I heard Madame Bree murmur, "You know him, Margot? The reason I ask, he is entered in my carnality contest. Do you think he has a chance?"

To my surprise, Mme. Metayer did not hoot with derision. Certainly that evening in my rooms at the Plaza-Athénée must have left psychic scars on her female soul. Yet she might have been remembering the performance I put on in the HECATE testing maze.

"Either he will make your other young studs look like fags—or he will be less potent than a hundred-year-old man. Professor Damon is a puzzle."

Sabine eyed me wonderingly. "So? One or the other? What is the key, Margot?"

"If you find out, tell me."

I flashed both women a smile and fled. I wanted to find Agnete Stralsund and learn a little more about this contest. I wanted to learn if Margot was to be among the contestants. I dearly wanted to get that bit of feminine fluff on top of a bed for a couple of hours, just to show her that the evening I'd insulted her had been a fluke.

Agnete was in the bar-kitchen, brooding over the remains of a sandwich. At sight of me, her eyes and lips flashed into a happy smile. She straightened up and cut off my excellent view of her heavy breasts in the scant bikini halter.

"Well! Will wonders never cease? I didn't expect to see you for an hour, at least."

"Sabine respected your rights as the owner of a contestant," I grinned. "She wanted me to hoard my manhood for when it would be most needed."

She slid off the counter stool with a flash of handsome tan legs. "First time I've ever known her to be so solicitous," she murmured. She came so close her breast tips

118

touched my chest. "What would you like to do?"

"Throw you down on the nearest cot and enjoy you," I said frankly, at which bit of honesty her eyelashes flickered, "but since I have to reserve myself for the contest, why don't you take me away from temptation for the rest of the day, the night, and tomorrow?"

"Good. I wouldn't mind some good clean fun myself. You have a car? Then we could drive into Copenhagen and I can show you the sights."

I pulled her against me and kissed her pouting red mouth. She let her thighs touch mine, her belly pressed me, and when the pudendal bulge at her bikini pants nudged my own bulge, her hips slid around and about in something approaching the bump and grind of a stripteaser.

"Now look what you've done," she breathed.

"Me? You were the cause of it." I kissed her soft throat, murmuring, "You're going to have to behave yourself, darling, if you intend to keep me chaste until that contest."

She pulled away hurriedly, shaking her mane of glossy black hair, parting it with her hands, thrusting out her tongue at me impishly. She was discovering how hard it was to keep me chaste.

"I expect a little cooperation from you," she giggled. "If the sight of my girlish body excites you so much, maybe I'd better wear a Mother Hubbard."

"You don't own one," I jerred.

She laughed and caught my arm and walked beside me out into the Danish sunlight, her hip and thigh bumping mine as a constant reminder of her attractiveness.

"I must pack an overnight bag," she was saying. "We shall spend all our time together, naturally. I don't want some hussy to get her hands on you and deplete you of your strength."

I did not bother to tell her this was an impossibility, since I was now safeguarded against my former radio-controlled impotency by the counter-stimulator the Thaddeus X. Coxe Foundation dentist had put into my tooth. And that was the only thing that could interfere with my satyriasis, which enabled me to play the stud male with unceasing vigor.

119

I like to surprise a girl occasionally. Agnete Stralsund was in for a very pleasant surprise, once that contest began.

"I gather that you and I are to perform together?" I asked. "While Hannie and Kaija and their young men will do the same?"

"Oh, yes, that's the way we do it."

A shadow touched her face. I did not understand that momentarily emotion yet, but I would before the contest was to begin, I promised myself.

"What about Madame Bree? And Margot Metayer?"

"They watch us. They and a third lady who comes with Sabine. A Madame Germaine Audibert. They act—like judges."

"What do they get out of it, except hot pants?"

Agnete giggled, but did not answer.

I clapped her soft behind with a hand, on the beach patio, telling her I would go get my Volvo and be back in half an hour. She promised to be ready.

She was standing in front of the beach villa, two bags at her feet, as I braked the Volvo to a stop. She wore a simple mini-skirted dress and beige nylons with ivory pumps. A Pucci scarf was twisted about her long black hair.

Happiness was a smile on her face as she let her head fall on the seat rest as I started off. "It's been a long time since I went out with a young man just for fun, and no games."

"Good. We'll keep it that way," I agreed.

The first thing we did in Copenhagen was rent two bicycles and go riding over the cobblestoned streets, past the neat house fronts and shop windows like any boy and girl on a date. We parked the bikes and went strolling on what is known as Copenhagen's "walking street," the Stroget.

The Stroget is lined with stores and shops. Tourists from all corners of the world come here for Georg Jensen silver, for Flora Danica tableware, for Royal Copenhagen of Bing and Grondahl porcelains. I bought a Royal Copenhagen statuette for Agnete, a shepherdess in straw hat and flowing skirts.

From the Stroget, we bicycled down to the waterfront along cobbled streets without a speck of dirt on them and

120

flanked by narrow walkways, to walk along the Langelinie Promenade from which we had a good view of the Little Mermaid crouched on a rock in the harbor.

Hand in hand we strolled through the streets until my stomach told me it was long past the time to eat. Agnete suggested the Seven Nations restaurant, where seven dining rooms are assigned to seven different countries.

We ate in front of a rock grotto, at a table where a miniature stars and stripes was planted. We feasted on roast beef with a bearnaise sauce, and flaming crepes suzettes. We toasted each other with Cloc whiskey and finished off the meal with Cherry Heering. It was a grand success, that dinner. Agnete was a laughing witch who completely captivated my heart, while I was at my very best as a raconteur of funny stories.

As dusk swam over the city, we left the Greenland Room, Agnete with her head resting against my chest, my arm about her middle. She had suggested as our next stop, the Tivoli Gardens and one of the two dance pavilions it boasted. I was in the mood for dancing, for holding her soft body close to mine as we moved to slow waltzes or faster fox trots. Even the fish or the bugaloo sounded good to me, if Agnete Stralsund was to be my partner.

I paid the one kroner admission fee (fourteen and a half cents) and wandered hand in hand with Agnete past the softly lighted fountains, tinted red and green and yellow by the many electric lamps. We paused in the shadows to kiss, we went arm in arm by flower beds that seemed to scintillate in the many lights.

We danced cheek to cheek at the pavilion that was Agnete's favorite—it played more romantic music than the other, she explained—and when I held her too closely so that she could feel for herself how she excited me, she wriggled away and chided me with glee in her voice.

"You must behave," she would breathe, snuggling her cheek to mine. "You must not get too excited."

"Are you worried about me—or yourself?" I wondered.

She drew away so she could look up at me. The shadow was there on her face. "What makes you ask that?" she demanded breathlessly.

I shrugged. "I am a professor, you know. I teach sex

121

techniques as an adjunct of my sociology courses. I am the founder of the League for Sexual Dynamics."

Her blue eyes were very wide, her bee-stung lips open. "You are not teasing me? Is this really so?"

"It is so. I informed your Madame Bree about it, in case she might want to disqualify me."

"Disqualify you? Oh no! What did she say?"

"She said she hoped I'd make her very happy, if I won. However, she doubted that I would. We even made a little bet."

"You didn't!"

I told her about our bet. We were dancing slowly to a romantic number at the moment, and as I whispered into her ear, I noted that she came crowding my body with her own. She was breathing a little faster too.

"You really think you can win?" she asked wistfully.

I hugged her closer, noting that her breasts had become hard. I began to think about Agnete Stralsund and the shadow on her face. I was reasonably certain she had a problem; I wanted to learn what it was, because suddenly I understood why she was always an entrant in the sex sweepstakes and never a winner.

"I'll win—with your cooperation."

She digested that, moving her hardened breasts against my chest. "What's that supposed to mean?" her voice demanded harshly.

"Don't be angry. I want to help you."

Her face was genuinely puzzled as she stared at me. "Help me? If you win the contest, you'll help me all you can't."

"Oh, the contest. I don't mean that. I mean this other thing, this coldness in bed which troubles you."

It was a long-shot, but I had years of sexual study, of contact with many girls and women with sex problems. I had studied Agnete Stralsund enough to understand a little about her.

She drew herself away, remote and inscrutable as we finished the dance. When the music stopped she headed for the edge of the dance floor with me in close pursuit. She was angry, but she was even more troubled.

As she threaded her way toward the walkway, I caught her hand and held it with sheer strength. I murmured, "I am not going to apologize. You know yourself even better than I do. You do have a problem. Without knowing any more about you that I do now—never having been to bed with you, that is—I can tell you it is your own fault you've never had a winner in those sex contests."

Suddenly she grated, "Damn you!"

"There's no need to be ashamed of it," I murmured. "Everybody has a kind of bag on about sex. It's not always peaches and cream. Believe me, I know. I've met and talked to all kinds of females."

Agnete turned her face toward me. Now I could see the angry tears staining her cheeks wetly. I drew her into the shadows and licked those tears off her smooth cheeks with my tongue. Her body was stiff, unyielding.

I whispered, "I like the taste of your tears. I will like the taste of your body too."

She shivered and moaned faintly. I was positive of my quarry then. Agnete Stralsund was a coprolaliast, aroused by the use of erotic language during lovemaking.

One more thing I was certain of: she was not a HECATE girl. She could never have faked her surprise when I revealed the fact that I was the founder of L.S.D. So I scratched her as a threat. She was not the spy sent to kill me if I failed to kill Madame Bree.

I drew her against me. The rigidity leaving her flesh, she pressed eagerly against me as I added, "I want to undress you, Agnete. I want to take your clothes off and kiss you all over."

Her moan was louder. She was panting in my ear as her hips began a slow, rotary motion that was completely unconscious. I drew away from her so abruptly that her face was almost grotesque in her surprise.

My hand caught her arm and moved her along the path. She came quietly like a little girl with a parent. Agnete Stralsund was not thinking too clearly at the moment, her body was feeling the stab of desire my words had roused in her.

"We aren't going back to my hotel room yet," I informed her. "I feel like dancing some more. Something wild, like at a discotheque. Are there any in town?"

"The Adlon," she murmured.

We went to the Adlon and fruged and fished for two

123

hours. The exercise put Agnete in a better mood, she was back to her hand-holding as we walked out into the street a little after two in the morning. I found a cruising taxi and told the driver to take us to the Kongen af Danmark hotel.

In my room, Agnete looked at me questioningly. "Now what is it about me you think you have discovered?"

"Not now, honey. Tomorrow at the contest. I want to take you by surprise. I want you completely natural. I don't want you thinking about what I might have told you."

She bit her lip and shrugged. She was accepting my leadership, no longer the trainer but the trainee. Half bashfully, she removed her nightgown from her bag and walked toward the bathroom. I did not stop her. Time enough tomorrow to see her nudity for the first time.

I got undressed and slid into bed. Moments later she came out of the bathroom and paused near the lamp on the night table. Her shortie-nightie was completely transparent, it showed the half-dollar-sized red nipples and the froth of ebony pubic hair at her loins.

My hand threw back the covers.

"Turn out the light and get in. We're going to sleep together and neither of us is going to get excited."

She stared at me as if not believing her ears. "You mean we aren't going to——"

"You want me to save myself, don't you?"

"Well, yes. But——"

"Then climb in here and go to sleep."

She obeyed. It was difficult to feel her softness against my body and not do something about it. I would have, gladly, but now I was keeping *her* chaste against the moment of her need.

Deep fires were banked inside this girl. A sexologist like myself could rouse them to fiery incandescence, but this was not the time. I must win that week at the Bree villa, it was part of my assignment. To do that, I needed a partner who would be as anxious to have me win as I was myself.

It was my firm belief that it was Agnete Stralsund who had failed the men she selected as entrants, not the other way about. A man needs cooperation and eagerness in a female for him to do his best. She must like—or appear to like—the things he is doing to her. Agnete had not been such a girl in the past.

Tomorrow she would be as eager as a nymphomaniac.

So I felt a soft, heavy breast brush my arm, knew the touch of a warm thigh flung over my legs, let her long black hair tickle my chest as she moved in her sleep, without so much as patting her backside. It was hard on me, no pun intended, but after a while I fell asleep too.

I had planned an itinerary for the morning and afternoon that would keep the two of us busy until it was time to set out in the Volvo for the villa.

We breakfasted on ham and eggs, *aiblekage*—apple cake—and coffee. Then we were off to Amalienborg Palace to see the changing of the guard, we visited Rosenbord Castle to view the crown jewels, we went to the Glyptotek museum.

At three in the afternoon, we stopped in at Oscar Davidsen's restaurant for a few of his hundred and seventy-eight differing types of open-faced sandwiches. It was only an hour drive to the Elsinore sands, and I wanted to arrive well fortified for the contest.

I was happy to see that Agnete was her old self. She bubbled laughter, she teased me about not responding to her almost-naked charms when she was in bed with me, she even pinched me from time to time. The shadow on her face was a thing of the past. She was convinced in her mind that I possessed the philosopher's stone that would enable me to win the prize.

We pulled onto the blacktop parking space alongside the Bree villa at quarter after five. Agnete explained that the contestants enjoyed a cocktail and a cigarette before being called into the contest chamber, and that everybody had to wear certain special garments. Giggling, she refused to tell me what either of us was to wear. All I could get out of her was the fact that Madame Bree changed them from year to year.

We entered the villa, hand in hand.

A pert blonde maid met us, escorted me to a small room in the lowest tier of rooms; it was like a bathing locker, where you could hang your clothes. It was empty save for a *cache-sexe* of transparent black nylon which was to be my only garment.

125

I slid out of my clothes and into the *cache-sexe,* then wandered to the bar-kitchen, where I found half a dozen other males sipping at martinis or manhattans or just plain whiskey.

Me, I ordered a *lemonad.* Whiskey dulls the erotic senses in a man, I have found. I wanted to be alert to every nuance. I asked for more ice in the tall glass, then settled back to await the arrival of the women.

Hannie came first, in a hip-length sheerness of red nylon. Kaija wore white, a redhead and a blonde were next, in blue and green, Agnete was nude under black nylon, and two blonde girls completed the list in purple and yellow. They were like flowers in their finery, I thought.

The young men who were their partners rose to their feet, their eyes taken by the beauty they were seeing, though perhaps not for the first time. I reached for Agnete, she came eagerly to my hand on her fingers and seated herself as demurely as she could in her black nylon transparency.

The girls drank cocktails too. By the taste of my lemonade, I knew something had been added, perhaps the tiniest bit of Spanish fly, to make certain we male contestants would do our best. Already our *cache-sexes* were bloating with the undeniable evidence of its effectiveness.

"You're not nervous?" I asked my black-haired beauty.

She shook her head, smiling, but she gulped at the Sazerac she had requested. I slid a hand along her thigh, saying, "Your skin is like warm cream, my darling. It will taste far better than your tears."

Her body remembered the way in which I had licked her cheeks clean of tears last night. Under the dark froth that was her sole garment, her nipples began stiffening. She squirmed a little on her chair seat.

A gong sounded. A couple of the most eager partners rose to their feet. The rest followed them. I was close enough to Agnete to touch her buttocks with my manhood.

"These are a better aphrodisiac than any cantharides," I told her, and moved slowly, back and forth. She flushed, gasped, and half turned to me.

"Walk," I told her, and glued to her behind, I followed

126

the others out of the bar-kitchen and up the flight of stairs.

I whispered as we walked, I told her she had the prettiest derrière I had ever seen, that her cheeks shook like brown jelly (they were as tanned as the rest of her) and that I could spend a day just examining them. She was gasping and nudging me with her flattered behind as we stepped through a heavy brocade drapery into the contest chamber.

There were seven beds in the big room. Each bed had a contour sheet on it, no more. Colored scarfs hung from each of the four bedposts. Agnete and I moved toward the bed with the black scarves.

A dais holding three chairs stood behind the beds. On each chair sat a woman in an evening gown. Madame Bree, Madame Metayer, and an unknown woman with very white skin and black hair flecked with gray, who was undoubtedly Madame Germaine Audibert, were here to serve as judges.

I gave Margot a mock salute. She stared back at me quite coldly.

Sabine Bree said softly, "For those of you who do not know our rules, there are five basic positions that must be attempted. The man-above and woman-supine, the woman-above and man-supine, the man and woman on their sides, the Venus reversa, where the woman kneels and the man takes her from the back, and the standing position.

"We will proceed in order as named.

"If at any time the man—or the woman, for that matter," and I saw her eyes touch Agnete, "cannot or will not continue, let them remove the scarves from their bed posts.

"If anyone completes all five of the postures, he will be adjudged the winner. If no one completes all five, he will be named winner who outlasts the others."

I heard a big blonde youth to my left breathing harshly. He was the partner of blonde Hannie. I glanced at them. Hannie was standing with her arms by her sides, but with the fingers of her left hand she was tickling her handsome companion on his bulging *cache-sexe*.

I raised a hand. Madame Bree glanced at me.

"How long do we have for each position?" I asked. "What I'm getting at is, we don't just act like a lot of animals, do we? Don't we have any time for love-play?"

Madame Bree smiled in delight. "Congratulations, *Professeur!* For the first time we have an expert in our midst, who understands something about the female body. Usually we have fifteen-minute periods. Suppose we extend them to half an hour, fifteen minutes of which must be spent in conjunction. Is this fair to all?"

Nobody argued with the boss.

I whispered into Agnete's little ear, "I want time to convince you how exciting you are, sweetness. No slam-bang, thank you, ma'am, measures for us. I want to kiss you all over. Everywhere. You must be convinced you are the most desirable woman on Earth. . . ."

My voice went on whispering even while the gong sounded that was to start the contest. As far as I was concerned, Agnete Stralsund and I were the only people in it. I wasted no time in watching the others. My job was to turn this girl with the long black hair into an unthinking animal.

I began by kissing her smooth tanned shoulders. I kissed her upper arm, off which I was lowering her shoulder strap. As I kissed I whispered words that only Agnete could hear.

"You are a love goddess. Astarte. Venus. Aphrodite. Your skin is wine caught in suspended animation. Your very sweat is like the amorous tears of all sensually tormented women. . . ."

As I have said, Agnete Stralsund was a person who must either talk or hear talk about erotic matters to get her kicks, to be aroused to the very utmost. She had failed at sex in the past because her partner had no consideration for her as a female. He was so bedazzled by the prospect of the five thousand kroner and the week at the villa which would be his reward, that he ignored her feelings.

Not me. My main concern was Agnete. She was the weak link in my chance at the week here in this villa. I could count on my priapism to see me through. Agnete had to go along with me, or my attempt would fail.

So I told her things that might make another woman

128

blush and pull away. Not that she didn't blush, she did. But the words I poured over her flesh while kissing her naked back down to her buttocks, while fondling her heavy breasts which were as hard as marble, drove her mad with desire.

"Venus herself would envy you these love jugs," I breathed, lifting and shaking her breasts. "They were made for the lips of your lover to nurse."

I bent, I took each rigid nipple between my lips. I played at being her baby until her breath scratched heatlines in the air. My hands were sliding across her hips, down toward her black pubic puff and around to the soft bulges of her quivering buttocks.

"Please," I haard her whimper. "Do me now. Oh my God, don't torture me any more."

But I kept on whispering, toying with the various parts of her body with my fingertips and my mouth until she threw back her head and wailed out loud. Her hips were bucking uncontrollably. Her breasts moved only lazily, they were so hard, to those bump and grind movements.

A bell rang.

To my surprise, every couple but Agnete and myself were already in the frantic motions of love. I let Agnete drop flat on her back, I knelt between her spread thighs. I searched out her femininity with a kiss, then moved to take her.

She accepted me like a demented thing, her naked legs locking about my hips, fitting herself to me in one wrenching thrust. I had very little to do except support her with my hands on her rump; she was all motion with her hips and buttocks.

My voice was never still. I went on whispering into her ears, telling her in graphic detail what I was doing to her, what she was doing to me. She climaxed five times in those fifteen minutes, she left marks on my shoulder when she bit me in her final spasm.

The woman-above position was a continuation of our first copulative conjunction. I merely flipped her over so my back was flat against the sheet. Agnete rode me like a wanton, eyes closed and mouth open, bouncing, swaying, rotating her hips.

I aided her efforts with my voice.

129

"This is how Andromache took Hector, her husband. Their servants used to watch them, you know. In Troy, during the Trojan War, it was her delight to ride big Hector, to feel as if he were bursting her tissues. She claimed . . . ."

Agnete screamed, doubled up on me, biting her lips to stop that instinctive admission of her sensual pleasure. My hand hit her naked hip, made her continue her movements atop me.

". . . . claimed she could feel more of her husband in this way. Go on, love. You are Andromache, I am Hector. You like the feel of my maleness filling your love channel, sliding back and forth. It stuffs you. It brings you such release as you've never known. . . ."

The half hour ended when a bell rang.

I swung my pussycat partner onto her side without breaking contact. My hips flailed away and Agnete counted her orgasms with her shrieks. My fingers were buried in her buttocks. I lay on my left side with my left arm under her moving hip, my right arm thrown over her. Like a dancing impressario, I guided her motions with those hands.

I threw one glance around the room.

Only one other couple remained in action, Hannie and her blonde boyfriend, but he was tired. His movements were slow, and his contorted face made me realize he was at the end of his rogering rope.

Madame Bree was crouched on the edge of her golden chair, staring down at Agnete and me with bulging eyes. Her evening gown skirt was drawn back above the tops of her sheer nylons. I could see that she wore nothing but her Merry Widow corset under her gown. Beside her, Margot was leaning back in her chair, eyes shut tight. Her soft thighs were moving, one against the other.

The third judge, the woman with the graying black hair, was licking her full red mouth, staring at us. Her hands were buried deep in her lap and her face glistened with perspiration. I wondered if she might be the HECATE woman sent to spy on me, even as I felt Agnete stiffen and shudder yet again.

The bell rang.

Hannie cursed in French, fluently. She rolled her

boyfriend off her, turned to stare at the bed where I was swinging Agnete onto her knees. Her black hair was hanging down, her heavy breasts dangling between the arms on which she rested, face down on the sheet, she was all set for a bout of Venus reversa.

I stared admiringly at her tanned buttocks a few moments before I stabbed forward. She groaned and arched to meet me.

There was no more need for talk. She was in a frenzy, in that state of ecstasy the Chinese name *yen* and the Arabs call *kayf*. She was utterly mindless, existing only at her erogenous zones.

Madame Bree shrilled, "Enough! You've won, *Professeur!*"

I cried out, "No, no. The contest calls for five figures of Venus. We shall enact them all."

My eyes sought out Margot Metayer, challenging her to decide once and for all whether I was a lover or an impotent humbug. My professional pride was at stake.

I heard Hannie mutter, "Go it, Damon!"

My lips flashed a grin at her. She smiled wanly in response, but I saw the look of pouting jealousy on her pretty face. She leaned forward saying, "Nobody's ever gone the whole way. Can you?"

Maybe she only wanted me to kill myself with a heart attack, but I could have been doing her an injustice. I used her facial expression and that of Margot Metayer to spur me on.

Agnete Stralsund was almost unconscious on her knees before me. Her head swung from side to side, she was mumbling incoherently. I felt the need to spur her to further effort so I snaked my hands about her, caught her hanging breasts and squeezed them until the pain got to her libido.

She came alive again, screeching, hips working savagely. She had caught the sheet between her fingers, squeezing it into balls of linen that she gripped as if for a handhold on reality. I do not think Agnete Stralsund knew where she was, right at that moment. All she could understand was the ecstasy feeding itself into her flesh.

Madame Bree was crying, "Stop them! Somebody stop them!"

131

Nobody moved. Everyone was hypnotized by the go-go action on the bed where the black scarves hung. Hannie was kneeling on the edge of her own bed, her eyes wide, her tongue licking her lips. Beyond her, Kaija was biting on a knuckle, eyeing us over her hand at her mouth. The others were in various positions of utter awe.

A bell rang for the fifth position.

I slid backward off the bed, I turned Agnete and lifted her. She could not move her legs, so I had to hold her by her bottom and rise to my feet with her body a dead weight in my arms.

The standing position—stasophallia—is known as the *el keurchi* position by the Arabs. It is the pose in which Milanion is said to have enjoyed Atlanta, just as Aloysia Sigaea relates how Tullia took La Tour while he stood imbedded in her, supporting her weight with his hands on her buttocks.

I began walking with Agnete about the room. I felt a little sorry for her, she had never been in this position before, so satiated with love-play that she could not move a muscle. But since I wanted to finish up my performance in a blaze of gonad glory, I began to talk again.

"Open your eyes, Agnete. Look around you. See how the others envy what you are enjoying? Ah, yes. You see? We are moving around the contest room, coupled together as Hannie and Kaija watch with jealousy in their eyes. And see Madame Bree on her chair, almost fainting with the need to enjoy what you are enjoying. . . ."

I got to her after a time. Her arms locked about my neck, she managed to grip me between her tanned thighs and fasten her ankles together. I put her spine against a wall in suspended posture of the Orientals, and fed her with my flesh until she spasmed, wailing. ⌐

I let her down gently. Her legs buckled under her and she slid to a heap at my feet. I turned and smiled at the audience.

My manhood was still at full strength.

Madame Bree moaned and slid off her chair, walking toward me in a daze. She came up to me, lifting her skirt above her corset. I think she would have asked me to take her at that moment, if Margot Metayer had not run to thrust her out of the way.

132

"Me!" Margot screeched. "I deserve him. He failed me once. You wait."

The shock of the interruption woke Sabine Bree to her senses. She drew a deep breath and pushed Margot as that lady was pushing her.

"This is my villa," she panted. "What I say goes, here! You shall wait, my dear. As a matter of fact, you'll leave the villa at once. At once, do you understand?"

She was getting hysterical.

I reached out and slapped her face. Hard.

"There's no need for over-emotionalism," I told her. "We have a whole week before us. Have you forgotten the terms of our bet?"

I thought she might round on me, clawing, but she was meek enough. Her eyes fawned on me as she nodded.

"Yes, a whole week. But not with Margot. I do not want her around. I insist upon it."

I wanted to teach Margot Metayer a love lesson, but I discovered that Sabine could be very stubborn. In the end, I shrugged my shoulders and spread my hands as Margot stared at me with her dismay clear to read in her eyes.

"I am sorry. You heard her. It cannot be." Then I added, "Perhaps another time, my dear."

She nodded, biting her lip. There was agony in her face, and I could guess at the frustration which must be eating in her body. Then a thought came to me. Could *she* be the HECATE agent who was to kill me if I failed to kill Sabine Bree? If so, her agony might be caused by the knowledge of what would happen to her because of that failure.

I really felt sorry for her.

And yet. I was relieved at the same time. If she was my fellow HECATE helpmate, I would have a free hand, here in the villa, once she left it. I watched her turn and walk away with conflicting emotions in my heart.

CHAPTER EIGHT

My job was to kill Sabine Bree.

It was also my job to satisfy her sex needs, by staying a week in her villa with her. Madame Bree made that plain enough, half an hour after Margot Metayer left the villa.

I was in the room assigned to me as winner in the carnal contest. I was staring out the window at the stars and their reflection in the waters of The Sound. I did not hear the door open, but suddenly I felt a hand on my naked back.

I still wore my black nylon *cache-sexe*. The covers had been turned down on the bed, and the bed itself looked mighty tempting. I was tired, my muscles ached from the use to which I had put my body. So when I felt the hand, my heart sank.

Sabine Bree was smiling at me. To my surprise, she was still dressed in her black satin evening gown. Her soft palm reached out, ran down my naked back.

"Tired?" she wondered.

"Not too tired. What've you got in mind?"

Her hand was on my lean belly, sliding downward toward the manhood she wanted. Her fingers were tickling feathers that became sharp red fingernails, scratching and soothing and rousing. I reacted to those female fingers as she hoped I would.

"Ahhh," she breathed. "You aren't too tired."

She was watching her fingers slide inside my black *cache-sexe*. I gasped to the touch of a soft, pampered hand that measured and fondled and toyed. Her breathless, excited laughter filled the bedroom. I thought sure she was going to suggest I bed her down.

Instead, she murmured, "Your flesh must be made of iron, my dear. But while your flesh is strong, your will is

134

weak, to paraphrase an old saying. I want your will to be just as firm in resolve as your maleness is firm in reaction. So we shall invite you to attend our bedroom-victory feast as an honored guest. A mere spectator."

This was fine with me, except for one thing. I am quite used to being a spectator at my League for Sexual Dynamics classes. I can control my reactions, if I so choose. I did not count on Madame Bree, who knelt to pull off my black nylon covering.

She wanted me stark naked. And while I was stark naked, the pert little blonde maid who had ushered Agnete and me into see Madame Bree yesterday afternoon was called upon to administer to my flesh, while Sabine watched the ritual.

The girl carried a sack of red powder, the same kind that the girls had patted on my flesh in the HECATE maze. The maid patted it on me, where it counts. I thought I might be able to get away with pretending indifference, but when the maid dimpled and held up a cup of liquid to me, I knew I was in for it.

The cup was filled with wine spiced by *datura stramonium*, one of the Solanaceae drugs. It is a poison, if given in large enough quantities. It is also a very powerful aphrodisiac. This thorn apple has been known to drive a man mad with unsatisfiable lust. It can also cause a man to maintain an erection for more than twenty-four hours.

As I sipped, tasting the thorn apple, I put the cup down and gave Madame Bree a hard glance. "I don't need stimulants, my body is able enough to please you."

"It isn't your body I'm concerned about, but your will," she smiled. "I want you to *want*, Professor! You're going to beg me to be good to you before the night is out."

She said, "Enough, Noelle."

The maid rose from her knees, her tongue sliding around her beestung lips. She was slimly curved, very pretty, with long golden hair falling about her shoulders and down her back. In a black maid uniform, equipped with white cuffs and a micro-skirt that showed off her shapely nyloned legs, she was really a bedable biddy.

Her somewhat slanted eyes flirted with me as she walked toward the door. Madame Bree knew what was going on, she stared from me to Noelle, and back again.

135

Her wise eyes told me that if I wanted Noelle, I was going to have to get her over Sabine's prone body.

"You're ready for the victory party," she smiled.

"I am? Like this?" I gulped, indicating my arousal.

"Of course, like that! You are Priapus. For a little while, you shall be worshipped as women worshipped the male principle in bygone days."

She turned and walked ahead of me, still clad in her black satin cocktail gown. She went on talking as she strode along. "You must be familiar with Knight's *Worship of Priapus?* And with Wright's *Discourse on the Worship of the Generative Powers?* Ah, I was certain you must."

"The cult of the god of the bedchamber," I murmured.

Her laughter was lewd. "Exactly. The rigid figure on which virgins sacrificed their virginity, on which matrons satisfied their lusts. In Egypt, the god Osiris was quite often shown with his membrum erect. His worship is tied in with that of the bull-god, Apis."

"Even the T cross represents the aroused male organ," I said.

She flashed a grin. "You are to be our Osiris. Or if you prefer, Priapus. Or the Roman Pan. You will be seated on a throne raised above the rest of the table. We women shall feast our eyes on your virility as we dine."

I have had women tell me that they worshipped me because of my unusual attributes. This would be the first time I would be enthroned as a deity, however. I found myself looking forward to the experience.

I was not forgetting my job as a Coxeman to dethrone HECATE. Before I could do that, I had to save Sabine Bree's life—and my own. I must discover the woman who was my fellow HECATE agent—and dispose of her in one way or another.

These thoughts were in my mind as Sabine Bree stepped aside, bowing to me, gesturing me to pass through a heavy curtain that hung in an archway before me. I put out a hand and thrust aside the brocade drapery.

I stared into a big chamber lighted only by the tinted flames of blue candles. The candles, no doubt chemically treated, gave off blue light. In that light, I saw men and women sitting at a dining table as naked maids moved here and there, serving them. The men wore the variously colored *cashe-sexes,* the women the tiny transparent shifts in which they had performed.

Seven women, six men. No, make that eight women, not counting Sabine Bree. I could see Madame Germaine Audibert in her cocktail gown, seated just below a large golden chair which stood empty on a dais at the far end of the table. The table appeared to float in the air, the shadows about it were very black and the bluish radiance was like something out of a horror movie.

As I stepped into the room, the diners rose and cheered. I was the victor, I was the god Priapus. I could hear the high heels which Sabine Bree wore as they followed the prints of my naked feet.

I stepped upward, seated myself in the golden chair. Instantly the diners reached for golden cocktail glasses. They lifted them and toasted me, the winner. There was no cocktail glass for me I was merely the symbol of the feast, the victor. I was a flesh and blood Priapus seated above the diners on whom they could feast their eyes and senses. An idol. The Mutunus Tutunus of the Roman bride.

They ate, a little below me, in the azure light. I could have been starving for all the good it did me. Madame Audibert sat below me to my left, Madame Bree to my right. I could stare down into their bodices at their large white breasts, if I cared to do so. Their bodices were wide and loose, affording my eyes a pair of double treats.

The young men and women who had been the performers in our fun fest were recovering from their exertions. I could see male and female hands wandering here and there on the all but naked bodies next to them. After a little while I gathered that Sabine Bree meant to tease me sexually until I was going out of my skull with lust. Then she would take me into bed with her and enjoy the end result.

Suddenly I decided that I would take a hand in the proceedings. I was still a Coxeman, I had a job to do—and maybe playing at Priapus would help me carry out my assignment.

I clapped my hands for attention.

Evidently this was just not done. No other winner in the

137

sex sweepstakes had ever indicated anything but complete cooperation with Sabine Bree. She turned a startled face up at me, she opened her mouth to speak. I beat her to it.

"The god will bless his followers," I announced.

She blinked her long-lashed eyes at me. She was curious, her stare was filled with interest. I do not believe she had the slightest idea of what was in my mind. Only one person would know that, if she thought about it at all.

"Come then, girls, all you who worship my sacred member," I called softly. "You, Hannie! Come here to the end of the table!"

The Danish girl giggled, got up on the tabletop and ran between the dishes and the glasses. My pointing finger bade her kneel before my boldly distended flesh.

"First, the kiss of worship," I smiled.

Eagerly she fell to her knees, leaned forward. I put both my hands on her smooth brown hair, letting my fingers slide over her skull even as her red lips opened and then closed about me. Her soft wet mouth was very skilled in this act of oral adoration. It almost made me change my mind about my plan.

I was too far committed to back out now, however. My fingers searched her head, found nothing. I sighed and leaning forward, put my hands under her armpits, drew her upward onto my lap.

My hands let her sink down on my straining flesh. Hannie rode me with delight glistening in her big brown eyes. Her hips pumped back and forth. When she cried out, I caught her suddenly boneless body and held her until she recovered.

"Kaija," I smiled, and held out my hands.

The blonde girl kissed my rigidity and was taken upon my lap. As I had done with Hannie, so I did with her. She erupted through her orgasm with eyes squeezed shut, her lower lip sunk deep between her teeth.

Her head formation was smooth, perfect. There was nary a bump on it to indicate a radio-control stimulator had been embedded there by HECATE. Scratch Kaija, as already I had scratched Agnete and Hannie.

To one side, Sabine Bree was glaring. She did not relish my abrupt dominance of the situation. Yet she said nothing. Perhaps she hoped that my acceptance of these girls would affect what she called my spiritual need for sex.

After Kaija, there was Joy, a petite temptress with purple eyes and hair such a pale platinum color, it was almost white. Her skin was as white as her hair, with a pearly translucence that made her seem unreal. She was anything but unreal, there was an imp of deviltry in her gaze as her teeth fastened onto my flesh and my fingers roved her skull.

She clambered onto my lap, but turned in the *kechef el astine* posture, so that I could watch the flesh-jiggle of her buttocks as she launched herself back and forth, up and down on the manhood that was my pride and her joy.

Daniella came leaping toward me as Joy slid away. I had watched her jumping up and down with eagerness, on one foot and then the other, while she watched the girls contort themselves upon me. She practically dove at me, murmuring to herself.

It is surprising how different women react to the sex act. There is the screamer, who shrieks and shouts in the intensity of her orgasmic frenzy; there is the silent weeper, who cries real tears as her body convulses in its spasm. Some women go acrobatic, bouncing this way and that so it is hard to keep contact with them. Others moan and groan and grunt, teeth set in their lips, while another category whispers or shouts all the obscene things she can think of. Some women just sit or lie there, inert and flabby, not giving anything of themselves at all.

Daniella was part acrobat, part moaner.

She mouthed me hungrily, her haunches wriggled ecstatically from side to side, she moaned deep in her throat. I think she derived as much enjoyment from being the donor of this philemaxenosistic caress as I did, myself, as its donee. She was sobbing softly when I drew her up on top of me. She threw her bare arms about my neck, she bounced like a pogo stick when she held me firmly planted inside her. She swung and looped and jounced as if she were on some sort of sexual trampoline.

Neither Joy nor Daniella were HECATE agents.

Elva was the last of the girls to come forward. She actually had to help me drag Daniella away. I think Daniella would have been content to ride me as her Hectorean horse all the night long.

139

By this time Sabine Bree had had it. Just as my hands were tangling in the curly blonde hair of the only girl whose skull I had not checked—Elva Zahler—Madame Bree marched forward. Her hands went out and caught those golden locks and tugged.

Elva was in the act of fastening her lips to my flesh when the older woman yanked. My fingers had to work fast, I could not put Madame Bree off any longer. I held onto Elva as the mistress of the villa pulled; between us we had a tiny tug-of-war; my fingers crawled like snakes over the girl's head, trying to find the telltale bump of a radio-control stimulator.

Sabine snarled, "Let her go!"

"Of course, dear lady," I replied, moving my fingertips this way and that under the golden hair. No bump so far. "I thought you wanted me roused spiritually. I'm only trying to get to that plateau the better to please you."

"I'll be the one to say whether you're aroused enough," the Frenchwoman snapped. "Now let go of her!"

"Mais oui, mais oui," I agreed.

My hands came loose just as *madame le general* gave a fierce yank. She went backwards, screeching, in tune to the yell that was ripped from the throat of Elva Zahler. I caught a glimpse of shapely nyloned legs, a garterclasp and a pallid thigh as her skirt split up its seam.

Sabine hit the floor on her behind and bounced.

To forestall an attack of hysteria, I leaped from my throne and lifted her to her feet. My arms went about her middle, banding her belly to mine. Her mouth opened to my kiss, and then her arms went about my neck. I was forgiven, especially when her thighs discovered I was just as priapic as I had been when I first walked into her victory feast.

"Quel homme!" she breathed, when she could.

Well, I had not found the girl whose duty it was to kill me if I failed to kill Madame Bree. In the back of my mind, I remembered the four maidservants who had waited on table as well as the blonde dish who had smeared the red powder on my manhood and given me the cup of thorn apple to drink.

I would have to examine their skulls as well.

Right now, I had other things to do, to placate Sabine

140

Bree and her friend Germaine Audibert. Germaine was standing, watching jealously as I kissed Sabine.

Into Sabine's ear I breathed, "Why not get rid of the others? Just you and Germaine and me. We'll have a ball."

She smiled lazily, patting my bare shoulder. "You're a naughty boy. You've spoiled all the things I meant to do here in this hall with you."

"We have plenty of time."

Her hands pushed at me. She was no longer angry, but she was determined to have her plans acted out. She explained I was here at her suffarence, that I must not make a mockery of what was, to her, a very serious rite.

My shoulders lifted in a shrug. If this was how she got her kicks—staging orgies at which a living man must pretend to be Priapus—then I would play along with her. Besides, I had not yet run my hands over her, or over Germaine Audibert. And it was necessary to my plan to get my hands on both these women.

I did not feel silly, sitting there. It may have been the blue light and the Stygian blackness of the rest of the room, the tall azure candles, the soft flesh of the girls and their handsome escorts, but the staging of the dinner was superb. I actually felt like a god, with all those eyes on me.

Sabine clapped her palms.

The entertainment was about to commence. The young men and the girls knew their roles, they stood aside and let the maids—there were four of these serving wenches, each one as pretty as the next—remove the tableware, the silver, and the glasses. While this was taking place, the performers were slipping out of what few garments they wore.

The table was the stage. The boys and girls made love to one another, while Mesdames Bree and Audibert and I sat watching. For me, a love-in is not a spectator sport, I much prefer to be a participant. But I went along with Sabine in her desires. My two days, which I'd won on a bet from her, would be coming.

I am afraid I yawned, after a time. The will was just not there. I was tired of seeing these girls and boys perform. If I'd had a part in the action, it might have been different.

Germaine Audibert saw my hand before my open

141

mouth, and gaped. She had been interested in watching the girl named Daniella and her boyfriend perform the *el nehati* movement of the Shayk Nefzawi. Wide as her black eyes had been then, they were even wider now that she saw how apparently uninterested I was.

"Sabine—he's yawning," she cried in dismay.

Madame Bree whirled on me, lips open in disbelief. "What's the matter with you?" she gasped. Her glance fell to my rampant manhood. "You can't be bored—not with that evidence of your interest so—so prominent."

"Priapus is priapic not because of these childish carryings-on—but despite them, my good lady. You seem to make the same mistake every other erotically inspired female makes. You think voyeurism will automatically inspire a male to venery. This isn't necessarily so."

"I believe him, Sabine," panted Madame Audibert.

"Oh, Germaine, do shut up," Sabine breathed. "Professor, what can I do—or should I have done—to excite you spiritually?"

"First, send the performers away," I suggested with an airy wave of my hand. I had already examined them and found them wanting. None of them was the HECATE girl spy who was out to kill me if I didn't kill Sabine Bree.

"The first rule of rousing a man is to offer him something new," I explained. "I've seen these people until I'm tired of them. Those four serving wenches, for instance —I'm saving you and Germaine for the finale, Sabine—together with that pretty maid of yours should be enough to get my tired old tendons into good working order."

Sabine raised her thin black brows. "It seems to me your tendons were never better. I think you're putting me on about something, but I can't discover what."

"Then why not find out?"

Her wise eyes studied me, then she nodded. *"Voilà!* I will do it. I will see what it is you have to offer me. Girls! Boys!"

Her crisp voice sent them packing. There were little protestations of annoyance, but Sabine told them they could stay downstairs at the bar and have themselves an orgy, if they wanted. They would be paid their full

142

bonuses, as well. It was just that Germaine and she wanted privacy with me.

Agnete blew me a kiss as she went out. Hannie looked back, laughed, and stuck out her tongue. Then they were gone and the two older women and I were left alone in the chamber lighted by the candles.

Sabine looked at me inquiringly.

It was up to me to offer *madame le general* something new and different by way of a sex gambit, one which she had never known, one that would have her climbing walls in her ecstasy. At the moment, I hadn't an idea in my head.

I dared not let Sabine know this, so I put a wise look on my face, caught her waist and that of Germaine Audibert in my arms and marched them out of the victory hall and toward a bedroom. Each woman was softly fleshed, expensively perfumed, each was a voluptuary, each had known the embraces of many men.

"The Hindu ritual of the stag and his herd of does?" I mused. "Or the Arabic twin temptations of the honeybee?"

"What are they?" Germaine panted.

"Postures by which a man may please two women at the same time," I explained. "Each person is involved, each posture affords the maximum in erotic pleasure. But since I want this to be an especially memorable evening, I've decided neither of those will do."

"But you have an idea—for another?" gasped Sabine.

"I do. I think we shall attempt the Chinese posture known as planting-the-geranium-bulb-in-the-twin-flower-pots."

Germaine stared at me glassy-eyed. "At the same time? Can it be done?"

"Wait and see."

We were outside Madame Bree's bedchamber. There was something I needed from my luggage if I were to indulge in the geranium-bulb-planting-in-twin-flowerpots. I explained to Sabine and Germaine that I would be back inside five minutes.

"No tricks," murmured the Frenchwoman suspiciously.

I grinned. I was as anxious to try the geranium planting

143

as she and Madame Audibert. I'd read of the posture but had never come across the opportunity to employ it.

"Be patient," I advised.

I opened the door and ushered them in.

Then I ran for my own room.

Among the erotic impedimenta I had purchased in certain shops in Paris—together with the penis splint I'd used on Margot Metayer in the Plaze-Athénée Hotel—was a lifelike replica in pink latex rubber of the male organ. This dildo was necessary to the proper technique for geranium planting.

ɩ Something moved in the shadows as I walked into my room. The lights were out; only the moonlight illumined the furniture and the unlighted lamps. The unknown girl from HECATE? Was she already in the room waiting to kill me? I doubted that she would strike so soon. HECATE was in no hurry. I had a week to spend in the villa, seven days in which to find a way to kill Sabine Bree.

I moved toward my luggage, threw open a valise.

Not by so much as a sidewise glance did I betray the fact that I knew someone beside myself was in here with me. Out of the corners of my eyes I had spotted that single movement. So when I leaped sideways, both hands flashing out, I caught the intruder by complete surprise.

I also caught her across the temple with a karate chop. Not hard enough to kill, just powerful enough to stretch her out unconscious at my feet. She gave a little squeal as the edge of my hand belted her, then she was collapsing into a tiny huddle on the floor.

It was the blonde maid, Noelle.

I yanked cordings from the window drapes, I tied her wrists behind her, and her slim ankles. I stuffed a handkerchief between her jaws and knotted it tight in her mouth with a third length of cording. I picked her up and dropped her on the bed.

She would be here, helpless, when I got back from my attentions to Sabine and Germaine. I ran my hands over her skull and in the cerebral cortex—the outer layer of her brain—just behind her right ear, I found the bump. Noelle was from HECATE. The stimulator in her head would compel her to kill me if I failed HECATE a second time.

Bound and gagged, this would be impossible for her to accomplish. I wanted to have a nice long chat with Noelle. But not now. Later.

Carrying the dildo in my hand, I walked toward Sabine Bree's bedroom. Pink straps dangled from the apparatus. I would tie those straps about my loins so that the lifelike rubber organ would appear to be a tail jutting outward above my backside.

The women were waiting for me, nyloned legs crossed, nervously smoking cigarettes. Their eyes brightened as I entered, my manhood as rampant as ever thanks to the aphrodisia powder Noelle had rubbed into my skin and the thorn apple drink. Their backs straightened, their hands went out to crush the cigarettes in ashtrays filled to overflowing.

"At last," Sabine breathed, eyes wide and worshipful.

Their eyes fell to the pink straps I was fastening about my naked loins. Understanding came to Sabine, she gurgled laughter and stood up, bending to catch her skirt in her hands and lift it.

"So then, I begin to comprehend," she smiled. "Darn clever, these Chinese."

"Unfortunately, the real *meche* cannot cope with the performance of the false," Germaine Audibert murmured.

"*Au contraire,* my dear," I commented. "It shall be a tie. You women shall be the first to call quits."

Her voice was muffled by the cocktail gown she was lifting off over her graying blonde hair as Sabine said, "Margot named you properly. You are a braggart."

"Want to bet?" I grinned.

She was sliding her arms out of the black satin gown, making an exciting sight in her Merry Widow corset out of which her heavy white breasts were bulging. The black garters bisected her plump white thighs, below which taut black nylons encased her handsome legs.

"I've already lost one bet to you," she laughed. "No bets. Just a performance to equal your words, that's all I ask of you."

I moved toward Germaine, putting my hands on her

145

zipper, sliding it down, baring her pale back. She was a beautiful woman, as Sabine was, and I ran my lips down her spine to the black of her garterbelt. She breathed faster, glancing back over her bared shoulder at me.

My hands pushed the evening dress down past her pallid hips, clad now only in the frilly garterbelt. Her hips were wide and firm, her buttocks pale and plump. She was somewhat slimmer than Sabine, but as she turned her body to step out of the gown, she revealed as large a pair of breasts.

I caught Sabine by a hand, drew her close, bending to kiss the white breasts poking out over the lace top of her Merry Widow. As I took their brown nipples between my lips, I heard her sigh. My hands were busy with Germaine, stroking her upper thighs and across her mounded belly into the ebony bush between her thighs.

Sabine and Germaine reached out themselves, they took my straining manhood into their fingers. Their caresses were gentle at first, but as my lips and hands roused them more and more, they became almost savage in their touchings. Germaine was whimpering, Sabine was sobbing softly.

I turned them, walked between them toward the bed. This was to be a complicated maneuver. I let Sabine sink down on the mattress and lifted her stockinged legs.

Her voice drawled, "If you don't last as long as your tail—I'll hate you to pieces, Professor!"

Then she grunted, lifting her pale hips and writhing as I stepped forward, entering her. Mechanically her legs locked about my hips, she raised her arms to put them about my neck. My hands under her buttocks eased her forward and upward and she sank down upon me.

I lifted her, turned.

Germaine was staring at the movements Sabine was making, her hips working back and forth on me, as her tongue came out to moisten her lips. I said to Germaine, "Lie down. You're going to have to guide me."

"Later we switch?"

I nodded, grimly determined to wear out these two sex-pots so that they would be soundly sleeping when I left the bedroom to go and question Noelle.

Madame Audibert positioned herself, thighs wide apart,

146

hand reaching for my tail. I backed into her. She guided the rampant dildo until it was deeply fleshed. She cried out, she danced her hips, she sent out her nyloned legs like snakes, seeking a hold on my body.

Sabine lowered her own legs without missing a beat, giving Germaine a chance to wrap her knees about my hips. Her arms banded themselves about my chest.

Then I stood up, the two women hanging on me, clinging like love-in limpets. Their hips were never still, they drove and looped and slammed, and I began my walk about the room listening to their soft cries of delight.

I could never take this posture on my feet. I needed help. I sighted a narrow vanity bench before the ornately mirrored table where Sabine Bree put on her make-up. I straddled it, sank down upon it. The bench was long enough to support both women and myself.

For half an hour we maintained the geranium-bulb-planted-in-twin-flowerpots position. Then Sabine wanted to try me from the back so the women disengaged themselves, exchanged places, and began again.

They moved three more times in the next two hours. I had begun to wonder if I'd met my match in these older girls. They seemed insatiable. Then I noticed that their heads were getting heavy. Behind me, Sabine was resting her cheek on my naked back; before me, Germaine was sinking her head on my shoulder.

They were almost asleep.

If I could come up with a real sexual smasheroo, I might exhaust them both. I ransacked my brains, my memories. There had to be a final bit of fiddle-bow fireworks that would do the trick.

The bride testings of the Kokah Pundit? That inspired epic of erotic enterprise, in which the fabulous Punditjee searches with an eternal erection for a female capable of matching his staying powers in *ruttee,* contained positions and postures enough to satisfy my needs. Then there were the fourteen erotic postures for three persons as related by Friedrich-Karl Forberg in his *Manual of Classic Erototology.*

None of those would do. I needed something special.

There was the Chinese wild-goose-seeking-a-lake-to-land-in, of course, in which one woman lies stretched on

147

her front while her fellow female reclines on top of her, face up. This presents the male with two targets at the same time, where he stands at the edge of the bed. But such a posture would give them rest, flat on their fronts and backs.

No, no. The women must do the work and—

Ahhh!

The feeding-of-the-baby-birds—a bit of Chinese imagery—might be just the medicine required. The man would lie flat here, the girls would be the ones using the energy.

I clapped Germaine on her rump. "Up! We're going to finish off our fun fest fireworks with a bit of Chinese fortune nookie."

Germaine blinked bleary eyes at me. Behind me I heard Sabine whisper, "I don't think I c-can take any more. Lover, you've been unbelievable."

"The two baby birds feeding," I cajoled. "You've never lived until you've tried that. Up, up, both of you!"

They protested, but they got off me so I could undo the pink straps of the dildo and toss it to one side. Then I lay flat on my back on the long bench. Both women stared down at my excitement which was still unabated. Germaine I drew upon my lap, face turned away and downward. The student of eroticism will recognize a take-off on the *kechef el astine* posture of the Shayk Nefzawi. There is a difference, however. In the Arabic mutual-study-of-the-buttocks position, the woman sits upright; here, Germaine Audibert lay flat, letting her breasts rest on the velvet top of the vanity bench between my calves while her hands gripped the edge of the bench.

Sabine straddled my hips, facing me, at the exact point where Germaine and I were joined. She stared down, she looked at me.

"I'm not part of it," she complained.

"You will be. Just trust the professor."

Germaine was moving her hips slowly, panting with the sensations filling her flesh. Sabine was resting her hands on either side of my chest, staring back between her legs at what her friend and I were doing. I took her dangling breasts in my hands, fondled and caressed them until she was breathing harshly.

148

Then I moved back and downward while Germaine cried out softly, and Sabine screeched as she sank down upon me. She rode me ferociously, for a little while. When she tired, I slapped the naked leg Germaine had stretched out beside my hip. The woman responded lethargically. She was exhausted.

When I was done with her, Madame Audibert was asleep. It was now Sabine's turn to be ridden to sleepy-bye time. It took about eight minutes before she collapsed on me, her body a limp, sleeping weight.

I slid out from under them, carried each woman to the bed, pulled the covers up over them, and turned out the lights. As I closed the bedroom door behind me, I heard the faintest of feminine snores.

Noelle was awake when I entered my own room. Her blue eyes were wide, somewhat fearful as she watched me close the door and advance across the moonlit room toward the bed where she lay gagged and tied. I switched on the bedtable lamp.

"Now then, we're going to talk," I smiled.

I unfastened her gag. To forestall a possible scream, I told her that I knew she was working with HECATE, and what her job was.

"For the record," I went on, "I want you to know that I do not intend to kill Sabine Bree, nor do I intend letting you kill me when I do not."

She digested my words, staring at me thoughtfully. At last she said, "I'm glad. I don't want to kill you. But, I'll have to. There's no way to escape it."

All too vividly I remembered my fight to escape from killing Henri Planget. I nodded my head. "Yes, it means I'm going to have to keep you tied up—until I can get a doctor to remove that radio thought stimulator in your head."

"HECATE would know—and stop you."

"HECATE isn't the all-knowing octopus you seem to think it." I smiled, and told her how I had outwitted Doctors Roger-Viollet and Matelot by using the hypnotic device. The more I talked, the wider her eyes got.

"If you could do that, you could hypnotize me too," she breathed. "You could make me think I had killed you. Then I wouldn't have to."

I had been thinking along much the same lines. But I had an even better idea. I would hypnotize her into believing that I had killed Sabine Bree. In that way, we could travel together back to Paris. I had even more than that in mind, where Noelle was involved.

I lifted the table lamp and moved it back and forth across her line of vision. Her eyes shifted, following it from left to right, from right to left, from left to right. I told her she was sleepy, that she must sleep and while she slept, she must put her confidence in me. She must tell me whatever I wanted to know.

Inside ten minutes, her eyes were closed.

She slept peacefully, quietly.

"What's your real name, Noelle?"

"Noelle Berlet is my real name."

"Berlet is a French name. Who were you in France before you went to work for HECATE?"

"I was the daughter of Pierre Berlet, Doctor Pierre Berlet," she answered dreamily.

"Doctor Berlet. Have I heard that name before?"

"You should have. He owned the hospital at Dampierre—before HECATE took it over."

I sat up straighter.

Maybe I was on to something, at long last.

CHAPTER NINE

I wormed the story out of her.

HECATE had sent its agents into the hospital some three years before. These agents had slowly taken over the administration, they practically ran the hospital before Doctor Berlet realized what was taking place around him. Berlet was an idealist, he enjoyed curing people of their ills, putting them on their feet again. He was a modern version of the Good Samaritan.

He had little head for business. He left such details to his assistants. One by one, HECATE assimilated those assistants, implanting radio thought-control stimulators in their heads. When the good doctor discovered what was going on, he wanted to go to the police.

Instead, he was overpowered in his own hospital, and was himself put under sedation that an electronic stimulator might be inserted in his head. He too became a HECATE agent, but he operated only in and about the hospital which he had founded and made a success of, to avoid suspicion of any hanky-panky.

They also operated on his daughter, Noelle, transforming her from a pretty nurse into an equally pretty secret agent. HECATE had given her assignments, she was intelligent, she carried them out perfectly. She had wheedled the plans for an atomic submarine improvement from a high-ranking French scientist, she had helped kidnap Rhea Carson, she had been one of a team of girl spies sent to England to involve one of their high officials in a scandal, she had been a good HECATE operative.

Her present assignment, of course, was to kill me.

"Do you hate HECATE?" I asked.

"Oh, yes! Of course I do! They stole my father's hospital. Instead of making its being a place where people are cured, they made it into a hellhole, where people are turned into demons."

"Would you like to see HECATE smashed?"

She drew a deep breath and her eyes filled with tears. "I would do anything, m'sieu—anything to bring that about!"

"Is there a secret way into the HECATE compound? I don't mean into the hospital, I mean into the maze quarters where their radio control gadgets are located."

"There is a way, known only to a few. I discovered it when I helped smuggle stolen monies into the compound. There is a vault located below the control room where they keep the funds they steal—and use in their devilish operations."

HECATE was a young organization, she told me, but it was fast growing. Originally French in character, it had been formed to aid the French during their Algerian troubles of the late Fifties and early Sixties—and it went on existing after it had been theoretically disbanded.

A few individuals, mad for power, mad for money, had used the tactics of the original HECATE group to gain control over one high official after another until those who might reveal the secret continuance of HECATE were all under HECATE control. This gambit had taken some little time to accomplish, but once it was a fact, HECATE began spreading its tentacles here and there in a world that knew nothing of its fantastic abilities to govern the minds of man.

There were Red overtones to HECATE, of course. When the DeGaulle government ousted the Reds who had infiltrated high government positions, HECATE struck back by taking over some of the men who most desperately fought the Communist invasion of French officialdon. While not outright Communist in all its actions, HECATE sympathized with the French Communists and sought to aid them.

Without relinquishing its grip on the men and women who served HECATE, however. Actually, HECATE was international in scope, or sought to become so. Within a

152

few years, HECATE might be the dominating force in the entire world. There was even talk of implanting control electrodes in the heads of men like Nasser and King Hussein of Jordan, several United States senators, and a scattering of English peers.

It was HECATE policy to embarrass American and English diplomats and cause their policymakers to appear incredibly inept. The attempts made by the United States to establish peaceful relations between Israel and the Arab countries were to be fought by forcing Rhea Carson—our only hope for such peace talks—to commit suicide.

Was the death of a man like Robert Kennedy part of a HECATE plan, involved as it was with Middle East relationships? Noelle Berlet did not know. It might be, she was not sure.

Thieves. Kidnappers. Assassins. This was HECATE.

It was an organization that was a real threat to world peace. A radio-controlled head of a government might easily egg such nations as the United States, Russia and Red China into a holocaust of war. It might also maintain the peace, if it served its own evil purpose. Noelle more than suspected that HECATE was behind the recent attack on the English pound and the American dollar. HECATE men had bought gold, pushing down its value.

Enough of HECATE. I knew its dangers. I had to concern myself now with the individuals who served it.

"Noelle, listen. This is your fellow agent, Rod Damon. I have just killed Madame Bree by smothering her with a pillow. Do you understand me? Madame Bree is dead. I killed her."

"Madame Bree is dead. You killed her," she murmured in her hypnotic trance.

"There is no need for you to kill me now. I carried out my assignment perfectly."

"No, there is no need to kill you."

"We are going away from the villa. Now—before the murder is discovered. In the dead of the night. Do you have much luggage?"

"Two bags."

"You will get them, carry them downstairs. Don't let anyone see you. You will meet me at the parking lot, and wait for me in my Volvo. I am going to phone Kastrup Airport, book passage for us both on the SAS lines to fly us back to Paris. You will come with me, like a good HECATE girl."

"I will come with you. My assignment is over."

"In Paris, you will do exactly as I tell you. You are under my domination. I am going to do what is best for you. You must not tell anyone, but I am going to free both you and your father from the HECATE controls that enslave you both."

"I will obey you. I hope you can do what you say." Her tone was wistful, like that a little girl promised the doll on which she has set her heart.

"You will wake when I snap my fingers. . . ."

In a few seconds, Noelle was stretching her shapely body in its maid uniform, her eyes wide and surprised at finding me sitting on the edge of the bed. To my amazement she registered outright disgust. Then I remembered that, while she was still a HECATE agent, deep inside her brain she was not a killer. She believed I had killed Madame Bree, and so she despised me.

"Get your things," I snapped. "We're leaving."

She rose and left the room.

Three hours later we were rising off the runway at Kastrup Airport, on our way to Paris. I had put through a call to Foundation headquarters. A car would be at Orly Airport to meet us and take us to an operating room.

Noelle Berlet sat subdued beside me.

She walked beside me through Customs as if she'd been doing it all her life. She made no objections to traveling with me in the big limousine that waited to pick us up. She even accepted the fact that she waas to undergo a slight operation without protest.

While she was under the knife, I slept.

Twelve hours later I walked into her room. There was a bandage about her head, but her blue eyes were bright with hope and her pouting lips curved into a smile at sight of me.

"I'm so mixed up," she told me. "What is going on?"

I explained the setup from the time I had rescued Rhea Carson from the car that would have killed her. By the time I was halfway through, she was sitting up in bed, clasping her knees, all attention. When I was done she came off the bed to kneel before me and kiss my hand. Tears were sliding down her cheeks, but her face was happy.

"You did it, you did it, you freed me," she babbled.

Embarrassed, I yanked my hand away. "We have a lot of work to do, Noelle. We're going to stage an attack on HECATE headquarters."

I made her get back in bed and rest, while I explained that the French police had been alerted as to what was happening. Fortunately Noelle had told me under hypnosis which of the French officials were tied in with the flics, so we had put them all under temporary arrest. The police were only too eager to cooperate. It had been agreed that many if not all the HECATE agents were innocent of the deeds they had been compelled to do; the radio thought-control stimulators in the hands of Yves Roger-Viollet and Cyrano Matelot were the causative factors; and so to save the lives of these innocent people, to prevent an out-and-out gun battle between them and the police, I was going into HECATE headquarters alone.

My job was to reach the control center—and destroy it.

Noelle reacted strongly to this news. "You must not! Don't you realize HECATE will know by this time that you did not kill Madame Bree—and that I did not kill you?"

I pointed out that I had no special time limit in which to kill the Frenchwoman. And I still had almost a whole week left to me at the villa. No, HECATE would not be suspicious. Until I appeared at the compound, of course.

"But if I can get safely inside, if I can reach the control room before anybody knows I'm there—we're home free."

"If," said Noelle softly.

I shrugged. It was a chance I had to take.

The Foundation organization in Paris needed two days to make the proper arrangements with the police. Noelle rested in her room, I slept and ate my meals in mine. We had to stay out of sight until the right moment.

155

Close to midnight on the fourth night after our arrival in Paris, Noelle and I were smuggled out of the Foundation building into a black limousine. I wore a black bodystocking with a broad leather belt that held a Colt revolver, half a dozen gas bombs and a few hand grenades.

I was a walking arsenal.

Noelle was to accompany me as far as the secret entrance to the maze buildings. Then I was to go on alone. It was up to Noelle to bring the police into the action when the exploding hand grenades told them the control center was being blown up.

If that signal never came, the police would know I had failed. In other words, I was dead. Then they would have to come in shooting and a lot of men and women who could not help what they were doing would be shot dead.

The limousine raced through the soft French night, past the lights of the boulevards and the occasional house lights where people were staying up late. In a short time, there were only the stars and a cusp of moon to watch our progress.

Finally the limousine stopped. Noelle and I got out. She took my hand in hers and led me along the roadway toward an abandoned barn. In the distance I could see the Dampierre hospital and the dark bulk of the maze buildings.

Noelle went into the barn. She did not have to strike a light, but went immediately to a barn wall and sought along it until her hand closed down over what appeared to be a simple wooden peg. She pushed the peg backwards.

A hidden panel in the wall slid back. I stepped through this hidden doorway into utter blackness. Noelle had coached me in the car. I know I had to take fifty-seven paces forward, make a right turn and continue along the subterranean underground tunnel for another two hundred and sixty-five steps. Then I would find a door barring my progress.

I would turn on my flashlight, and see a combination lock before me set into that door. The combination was 36-28-47. If I dialed those numbers, the door would open.

Ten minutes later, the door opened into a metallic corridor I recognized as being part of the mazework system.

156

I ran along it swiftly, congratulating myself on my good luck.

I turned a corner.

One of the HECATE guards, a big, muscular man with the moon device on his uniform, stood there gawking at me. I had one advantage over my Herculean opponent. I was expecting trouble down here. He was not.

I hit him across the temple with the edge of my left hand. He grunted and his knees gave way. I had no time to tie him up, so I belted him a second time, making sure he would stay unconscious for a good ten minutes.

I ran on. It could not be far to control quarters. I must find a stairs and—

Whoops! Hold everything, Damon.

Jeannette Lons had told me about the changing of the guards. She had said that the night watchdogs came on at one in the morning, and that they made their rounds and then took up their positions about two. My wristwatch told me it was now twenty minutes past that time.

The guards should be at their positions.

Yet here they were—I counted nine of them at a fast glance—walking along the corridor right at me. There was no place to hide. It was a little late for that anyhow.

Eighteen eyes widened at sight of me.

They all recognized me, and I guess they all knew I was not supposed to be here in this corridor with them. Maybe they didn't know my assignment, but one thing they were damn sure of. It was not here.

All nine of them came for me.

I turned and ran. As my feet pounded along the floor, my mind assured me that the game was up. I would never be able to get through to the control room now. The only thing one of the nine guys racing along after me had to do was walkie-talkie the alarm up to the control room.

My head swiveled. No walkie-talkie, for which I was grateful. But there were intercom phones scattered here and there in the maze tunnels. Let one of them detach himself from the others and pass the word along and I was d-e-a-d, dead.

There was a purple door in the wall up ahead of me. I hadn't the faintest idea where it lead, but it was better

157

than being out here with the guards. None of them had reached for the revolvers hanging in holsters at their hips as yet. I guess they figured I couldn't escape and there was enough of a sadistic streak in each one of them to make them want to take me with their bare hands, after slapping me around for a while.

Bloody and bowed, I would be dragged before Doctors Roger-Viollet and Matelot to take the punishment due me. I remembered how one HECATE agent had suffered in the maze compound. Jeannette Lons had related how he had taken two days to die, slowly roasting to death.

None of that for me, thanks. Not if I could help it anyhow. My hand went out to the knob of the purple door. I twisted the knob, threw open the door and stepped inside.

Lights flashed on in a room where the great guru god Psychedel was holding court in his own chamber. Wow! Green and red and purple pigments slashed and slapped across walls and floor and ceiling—slowly twisting and turning, colors running into one another so that my stomach began to taste nausea as I looked.

I could hardly stand up, let alone see.

I closed my eyes. I was back in friendly darkness.

Whirling, I ran my hands blindly over the purple door. No knob. Good! The guards who would be crashing into this room any second wouldn't be able to get out this way once they were inside.

With my eyes still squeezed shut, hoping like hell there weren't any traps in here, I bolted across the chamber. On the other side, I ran my hands around. No doorknob. No door, even. I got a bit panicky at this point.

My whole assignment was going to come to a thuddingly dull stop right here. I would be killed, HECATE would go on to rule the world. There wasn't any way out.

Then the door opened. I felt a draft of air, and opened my eyes. One, two, three, four, five guardsmen came racing into the room. The door slammed shut behind them. They had their eyes closed, too, being reasonably familiar with the room.

Come on, Damon! Think, man!

Ah, yes. My hand went down to my weapons belt. I

grabbed a can of slippery white powder similar to the Rio-Trol used by police to send rioters skidding and slipping on city streets and sidewalks. My finger hit the button.

I crouched down to send that skid-power outward. It coated the floor, it foamed among the the tints moving so maddeningly. As the booted feet of the guards touched that slip-stuff, they shot out from under them.

You can have trouble just standing up with this stuff under your shoes. Those guards never had a chance. They went flying every whichway. And the best part of it was, they wouldn't be able to get up. They would keep on slipping across the crazily colored floor until help came.

I whirled, standing in the one clean patch of underpinning left. My hands went here and there, they felt a crack. There was a door here. I did not open my eyes again after that one quick look at the Rio-Trol and the skidding guards. My hands would do the seeing for me.

Ah, here. The doorknob.

I turned the knob, stepped into the next room.

At least, I extended my foot. And my foot went into water. I yanked my foot out fast and took a look, never letting go of that knob.

The entire room was a pool of water. And swimming around in the water were a hell of a lot of deadly fishes, that grow from four inches to two feet in length. The hairs on the back of my head stood straight up.

Piranha! Or *serrasalmus rhombeus,* if you like.

The piranha fish comes from South America where it lives in the rivers of that continent, and is known for its bloodthirsty voraciousness. It possesses teeth as sharp as razors and an unholy appetite for human flesh. A horde of piranha fish will eat a living man who has fallen in among them in a matter of minutes, leaving only his skeleton.

This pool was filled with them!

Dazed by my discovery, I let my eyes slide upward. Well, at least HECATE was still in character. It had baited its trap with members of the characin fish family, but it had furnished a way of escape to an agile man. A number of ropes hung here and there from the ceiling.

Confidently I let go of the doorknob—the door slammed shut behind me as I did so—and leaped for the

159

nearest rope. I would make like Tarzan and swing from rope to rope as I crossed safely over that grim pool.

Unfortunately the rope began to rise. I say unfortunately, because while I thought at first HECATE was being real nice about this and was elevating me to a good, safe position near the ceiling, the rope never stopped going up. It was being pulled by a powerful motor and pulley, against which my muscles were useless.

My palms were getting rope burns from the friction as the rope was dragged up through my hands to disappear into a round opening in the ceiling. I could not hold it, and in a few seconds the rope would be gone and the law of gravity would send me plummeting downwards into the pool. I would splash and—

That would be the last of me.

My flesh prickled to the thought of hundreds of razor-sharp teeth eating me alive. I felt like being sick, but I didn't have the time for any such luxury.

I let go my rope, reaching for another.

I breathed a sigh of relief as my hand fastened on a length of twisted hemp. Then I realized the rope was sliding downward! But slowly, to give a guy time to study the little fishies in the pool swimming about waiting for their meal to come down to them.

My imagination made them all appear to be looking up at me hungrily. Does a fish's mouth water? If I ever got the chance, I determined to ask that question of a qualified ichthyologist.

I went to the next rope. It moved neither up nor down, it just stayed where it was. It figured. HECATE was devilishly cunning. It knew nobody could cling to this rope forever. Sooner or later his muscles would weaken, and he would be forced to let go.

At least, I had the opportunity to study the piranhas and the pool where they swam. Then I noticed something. Here and there, parts of the pool were free of the fish. I had a bad angle to study those fish-free sections, so I went down a little on the rope, hand under hand.

I grinned with sheer happiness.

Solid glass pillars, that's what they were. No wonder those piranha punks weren't swimming there. There must

160

have been eight to a dozen of those solid glass columns rising up from the bottom of the glass-lined pool. Almost invisible, thanks to the clearness of the water and the horde of fish swimming back and forth in there. About a quarter-inch of water washed across their tops so that the pool surface was unbroken.

I began to swing the rope back and forth.

When I was right over the top of a glass pillar, I let myself down. My body-stockinged feet were awash in cool water, but the piranhas could not get at them. There wasn't enough water for them to swim in, thank God! I just stood there breathing, happy to be alive.

My nerves needed time to quiet down.

There were four more guards somewhere in this maze, searching for me. Maybe they had even alerted the HECATE bosses. I doubted this, because if Yves Roger-Viollet or Cyrano Matelot knew I was in here disobeying orders, either one or both of them could never resist the whim to talk to me over the intercom.

I thought about Noelle Berlet and the police, waiting for my signal. Well, I was in no position to signal. I had all I could do to find my way out of this damn maze.

There was a maroon door on the other side of the pool. My eyes dropped from it along the water, hunting out other glass columns. I found them, after a time. They were arranged like stepping stones, but in a zigzag pattern.

I extended my leg, gathered up my courage, and stepped.

One foot put its weight down on a glass pillar, then the rest of me was standing there. The piranhas were growing frantic, seeing their nice, juicy meal getting away. The hell with them!

Two more columns, and I was home free. I stepped onto them gingerly, afraid I might get dizzy and fall off. I made it. The last column was right in front of the door. I reached out, turned the knob, and stepped onto the sill as the door opened.

I damn near fainted.

A big black leopard was crouched in the next room, green eyes sparking with the lust to kill. We froze, man and beast, me with a foot on the sill of the doorway, the

161

leopard flattened down, head low, tail a quivering length of black fur. Its leg-muscles were bunching. It crooned to me, deep in its throat.

The leopard sprang, a black weight hurtling right at my chest, claws out and poised to sink into my tender man-flesh. I yowled.

I could not help that cry that burst from my throat. I figured I had been through enough in this labyrinthine compound. The cry came out of me in a burst of frantic sound while that ebony cat was flying through the air.

I could not go forward—nor backward. I was pinned there in the doorway, bait for the claws coming at me. I squeezed my hand tight on the doorknob I still held, until my hand-muscles ached. Then a brain rain washed over me.

Idiot! The answer was right there in my palm.

My right hand tightened on the doorknob. My left hand went up to clasp the top of the door as I kicked against the door, coming off the glass pillar. The door opened outward over the pool with me clinging to it with all my strength. I hung there like a babe in its mother's arms.

A black fury went screeching past me, through the air.

All this happened in about half a split second.

I turned my head, wincing. The black leopard hit the water with a titanic splash. It screamed once, then it was deep under the water and those pool waters were reddening with its life blood.

The leopard struggled. I could see its twisting, heaving, body as it sought to rip free of the teeth slashing it to its skeleton. I felt pity for the beast, it was only doing what came naturally to it, by attacking me. My pity for the animal turned to hate for HECATE.

I snarled, staring at the red waters.

In a short time, a skeleton was sinking toward the bottom. I let out my breath, kicked the wall and swung back on the door over the bloody pool. My bare foot hunted the door sill, then I was sliding free of the maroon door and balancing myself right on the edge of that damned death-pool.

I slammed the door shut behind me.

The room in which I stood was empty, of course. Its

162

walls were painted to represent the flora to be found in a jungle, to make the leopard feel at home, I suppose. It also served to disguise the door on the other side of the room in case the man who came in here was lucky enough to avoid the black cat. By the time he found the door, the leopard would have him.

I needed time to use my think tank. I was reasonably certain where I was, deep in this lethal labyrinth, in relation to the overall compound. The time I had spent with Jeannette Lons in studying this maze was paying off big dividends. I fashioned an imaginative picture of the connecting rooms and spotted my position on a mental map.

There was another room beyond this, and on the other side of that was a kind of lounge room where the guards would be waiting to congratulate the HECATE-hero who might have passed through those barriers. Either that, or they would be marking time until it was safe to go in and recover his dead body. I had a feeling the four guardsmen who had separated from their five fellows would be waiting for me there. With drawn revolvers, yet.

My immediate problem was—

What was waiting for me beyond the next door?

I drew a deep breath. No use standing here. I had to keep going or let HECATE win this battle. I put a palm on the flowered doorknob and turned it.

I walked into a chamber with white walls, pink ceiling, and a red floor. The colors are unimportant to the action. What was important was the fact that the floor dropped an inch under my weight—and the side walls started moving together, with me in the middle.

I gulped and stood like a statue.

Those walls would crush me to death when they met!

Still, HECATE always played fair with the candidates it tested, so I guessed there might be a way out of this death-room. My job was to find that means of escape before those walls found me. I ran around the room, hoping the red paint covered a hidden switch that would stop those walls in their tracks. No such luck.

I knelt down on the floor before one of those moving walls and slipped my fingers into the inch of space between wall and floor, searching for a switch. My fingertips went all along the under-edge of the wall before it dawned on my hopeful mind that there just wasn't any switch down there.

Maybe it was on the other side of the second wall. By this time—I'd had to move backward as I fumbled around—the two walls were about ten feet apart and closing in.

I raced to the other wall, knelt down and began feeling along the under-wall. Nothing here either. Now the walls were five feet apart. Four and a half feet, four feet, three and a half feet, three feet.

My face was wet with sweat. I had no time left for thinking. It was act, man—or die. And I had to act right.

By reaching out, I could touch both walls. If I were Hercules or Samson, I could stretch out my arms and keep them from closing by sheer muscle-power. I am considered a strong man, but not that strong.

However, thinking of Hercules made me think also of Antaeus, son of Terra, a great fighter and wrestler who derived his great strength from contact with the earth under his feet. Hercules had finally beaten Antaeus by lifting him off the ground and into the air so his strength could not be renewed. Hercules had strangled Antaeus, but all I needed to do—

Idiot! Dope! Dumbkopf!

The answer was so obvious it was ridiculous. The entire floor was a switch. When I had stepped on it, I'd triggered off the mechanism that moved the walls together. Theoretically, by getting off the floor, it would return to the "off" position and the walls would slide back to normal. And while they were doing that I could sprint to the striped door on the far side of the room, open it and step through to face the four remaining guards.

I jumped upward off the floor.

I heard a click. Instantly the walls stopped their forward progress and began to recede. I landed back on the floor, naturally, but the mechanism could not reset itself until the walls returned to their original, at-the-end-of-the-room position.

I ran for the striped door before that could happen. My hand fumbled for a tear-gas bomb hanging at the broad

164

black leather belt buckled over my body-stockinged self.

With my left hand I opened the door while my right got ready to hurl the bomb. Just as I let it go, I would duck away from the bullet-rain coming my way from the guards' guns. This was my fight plan.

But as I saw the guardsmen in the lounge room, I knew I wouldn't have to duck. Oh, the four men were there all right.

One of them was sound asleep on a leather lounge. Two ohers were playing chess. A fourth was slumped down in an easy chair, legs crossed at the ankles, dozing.

A chessplayer lifted his head and stared at me. I have never seen such a grotesque expression of surprise on any face. His jaw dropped, his eyes bulged. His opponent seeing that face, turned his neck. He got a look of astonished awe on his features.

"Sacré bleu!" shouted the first man. "It cannot be! Nobody could go through all those rooms and live!"

As if he felt called upon to explain this, his fellow chessplayer said dully, "It was a new course. HECATE hasn't used it yet. It was to test our finest operatives—but HECATE hadn't figured out how to install safety devices without weakening the impact of the testing ground."

Those words came out in a rush. Both men were thinking their thoughts out loud in their amazement. The man in the easy chair was sitting up by this time, staring around with bleary eyes. Apparently these four had been waiting until it would be safe for them to go in to recover what they believed would be my dead body.

"Surprise," I yelled, and hurled the bomb.

I slammed the striped door shut on the hiss of escaping gas. While I waited there, I slipped on my gas mask. I gave the gas a few more seconds, then I opened the door and walked in on them.

The man who had been sleeping was kneeling beside his couch, bent over and retching. One of the chess players was clawing at the far door, trying to open it and get out into clean air. The other two guards were staggering about, sobbing and wiping at their tear-wet eyes.

I leaped into the room.

One man I belted with an uppercut to the jaw, the second I rapped across the temple with the edge of my hand. They dropped to the floor and lay there motionless.

The man by the couch, I ignored; he was too sick to be in on the action. But the man at the door I yanked back with a hand tight on his uniform blouse, turned him slightly and let him have it right across the cheekbone.

His head cracked hard into the door, his mouth opened and his eyes crossed. Spine to the door, he sagged downard. I had to pull him out of the way before I could step over him and out into the corridor.

In the hall I removed the mask and took half a dozen deep breaths. The mental map my mind had made back in the room of the leopard served to position me. I was about a hundred yards from a big chamber where the initiates into HECATE underwent certain tests so Doctors Roger-Viollet and Matelot could learn their reactions to orders flashed to the radio thought control gadgets implanted in their heads.

I figured nobody was being tested this early in the morning. It was close on to three o'clock. I ran down the corridor, loosening two hand grenades at my belt.

I skidded to a halt. I had been wrong about the testing chamber not being used. I had almost gone barging right into that brightly lighted room which was filled with a lot of naked men and women, all HECATE agents, taking part in a kind of orgasmogenic orgy.

I backed off slowly, hoping nobody watching from the control room had seen me. My black body stocking was great for running around in the dark night, but it would betray me instantly to the eyes studying the love-in at the control screens.

Beyond the room I saw another archway and through that the stairway that would lead me to the second floor where the control room was located. I had to get across the open space of brightly lighted space without arousing suspicion.

I swore under my breath. It was an impossible task.

Sure, I could have tossed a gas bomb in among the naked boy and girls—but I could never get across the room without being seen where it counted, in that control room. They'd be waiting for me up there with machine-guns.

I stayed in the corridor and studied the revelers. Something struck me suddenly. I knew most of the girls. They were nurses at the hospital!

Apparently HECATE was enlarging its forces. Until now, the nurses had been only that, nurses who worked there for a living. But I guess HECATE figured there was no reason why they should not accept them into the organization too.

The nurses had been operated on. Each pretty head in that room held a thought control gimmick embedded in it. Those gadgets were being tested now, by Doctors Roger-Viollet and Matelot. The nurses were being compelled to engage in this orgy so their actions and speed of response to the embedded stimulators could be studied.

Then I got an idea.

If I shucked out of my black body stocking, maybe I could take part in that love-in long enough to reach the staircase on the other side of the room. I had to have a partner for the task. I had to use her body to hide my face from anybody who might be looking from above.

Oh, yeah? What would happen when one of those nurses saw me? She would let out a yip of surprise, and catch the attention of the men watching the love-in.

I had one desperate hope.

My eyes ran around the room, past the twisting, pumping bodies which were engaged in a variety of joy rides, from the favorite European position of the woman supine to the more acrobatic variations. In a far corner, a woman was riding rantipole on a man stretched out on his back. It was like looking at an illustrated sex manual come to life.

I studied the nearest pair of lovers. They were busy with the *nik el haddadi* of the Shayk Nefzawi, except that the man was not adding the refinement of *sferdgeli,* which is likened to the blacksmith plunging a red-hot iron into cold water. I stared at them a little harder.

I knew that female body bent before the male. It was my little French sweetheart, Jeannette Lons! So they had made a slave out of her too! I felt hate rise up in my throat like bitter bile.

HECATE would pay for doing that to her, I vowed. Then my lips twisted in a grin. Why not use Jeannette herself to make them pay? She was within easy reach.

If only their position was such that her body could hide the face of her companion, it would be easy.

First things first. I stripped naked. I grabbed up two hand grenades, held them firmly in my palms with my fingers wrapped around them to hide them. All this time I kept my eyes glued to Jeannette and her lover-boy. He was taking her now in the Ninth Manner of the Arab erotologist. She was leaning the flats of her palms against the wall to maintain her balance as he drove into her in the *Venus reversa* posture. This was a delightful way of making love, but it exposed the face of the man, and I had to have some way of masking my features.

As I watched, the man drew back, Jeannette turned, thighs still parted. The man swung about, feeling with his back for the wall to brace himself against the standing St. George posture.

He was less than a yard away.

I reached out, caught his head, yanked him back. My hand belted him on the side of the jaw. We were inside the archway, there was no way the man or men at the control screens could see us. My hands caught him as he fell and lowered him gently to the floor.

Jeannette goggled at me. I warned her as I stepped forward to take the place of her unconscious partner, "Don't talk! Act natural!"

She was waiting to be swept into the woman-above erotipose. I braced the small of my back to the wall, I took Jeanette across my thighs, letting her sink down slowly onto my manhood.

"What are you doing here?" she gasped as I let her ride me as Andromache was wont to ride her Trojan hero-husband, Hector.

"No time to talk, just act," I grated.

I pushed away from the wall, my face between the bobbling white breasts that shook so richly beside either cheek. I pressed my lips against the inner slope of one jiggling breast, and then the other, the better to hide my features from the onlookers in the control room. Jeannette Lons did not bother to ask questions, she was too busy grunting in pleasure as I stepped between the bodies on the testing floor.

168

Under the soft buttock cheeks pressing into my hands, I had my fingers crossed. If I could make it across the room, if I could gain the archway door and the staircase beyond, I might still carry this off.

I had to make sure those watchers in the control booth did not notice me and so direct their attentions at this one male among all the others who seemed to be pursuing an independent course. Actually, by HECATE thinking, I was just a flesh-and-blood robot down here, performing for their amusement, no matter whether they called it initiation or nurse-testing or whatever.

If Roger-Viollet should see a man wandering around the room with his love-in lady when he was supposed to be crouched with his back against a wall, all hell would break loose. I intended that to happen, but in my own good time. So I walked on eggshells across the floor, expecting at any moment to hear the voice of doom crack out like thunder.

All this, of course, while Jeannette and I were doing some dirty work at the crossroads of her thighs. I was in this thing up to the hilt, and I kept hammering away. She was slowly going wild with my priapic performance, grunting and crying out, slamming her hips down and up in a steady rhythm.

I guess the guy at the control switches was too busy looking at what was going on around me to notice my pussycat pilgrim's progress. There was a couple, as a for-instance who were performing the *yumha'ee,* where the man squats down and the woman holds him between her widespread thighs, a position not so tiring as some for the male. Another duo were joined in the *neza el kous* of the Arab. This rainbow arch posture is performed with the woman on her side and the man likewise on his side but with his face toward her back. The female, gripping his ankles, bends his legs to make of his body a living arch.

Since all these couples were acting under mental controls, I wondered at the identity—and imagination—of the man directing them, as a puppet-master might pull the strings for a Punch and Judy show. In my own case, I realized that the radio stimulator in my head was causing me to perform this *el keurchi* rite, but the counter-pulsations of the gadget in my tooth enabled me to act independently of it, if I so desired.

I stepped over squirming bodies and between them. I made slow progress, but the archway was close now. And then, as if the Fates were laughing at me—my radio control gimmick started giving me new orders.

Kneel down! Take the woman from behind!

Apparently Jeannette was getting her orders too, because she pulled free of me and turned, dropping to her hands and knees. I dared not disobey those mental commands. The watcher in the booth wanted the fashion of the ram, so the Arabic *el kebachi* he was going to get. However, I dropped my head so my face would be turned away from the control booth.

Jeannette was there before me, plump white buttocks quivering. I realized that my face must be visible to the whole world, right about now. My only hope was that having ordered the change of position the director of this voyeuristic velitation would forget about me. Swiftly I moved into position, still trying to hide my face.

On my knees, my head was bent so far over that my cheek rested on her back. I nudged Jeannette forward. She slid a little on her knees, she advanced her palms along the floor to maintain her balance.

Had the watcher seen the grenades in my hands? I'd tried to hide them by keeping my fists close to my thighs until the blonde nurse was in position. Then I'd tucked my hands under her belly.

I wondered if anyone had ever enjoyed sex under more unusual circumstances. For I did enjoy it, even while a part of my mind was going fast enough to break a mental Mach One. My body was hammering away at Jeannette, forcing her to squirm forward toward the doorway to the control room at every delightful thrust. While I pumped sex, I planned strategy.

The French girl and I were performing the *tachik el heub* motions of love which added to my thrills. In this, the male member is thrust inside the vaginal passage to the root. It is never withdrawn, the man just keeps hitting the woman with his hips. I had chosen this particular method because I had to cover ground, even while I was covering the blonde

170

nurse, and this boxing-up-of-love motion seemed the only one applicable to my needs.

I could reach out and touch the archway jamb.

My hips danced a fandango and Jeannette Lons screamed, hips bucking wildly even as she lost her senses and fell face down on the floor at the foot of the staircase. I knew she was out cold from too much phallic action too fast.

From my vantage point behind the moaning girl, I could not be seen from the control room. I got to my feet, loosing my hands on the grenades, and went up the stairs two at a time. The door to the control room was ajar.

I paused to pull the pin out of the grenade in my right hand. I counted five, then my shoulder hit the door and sent it swinging. I paused in the opening, right arm cocked.

Doctor Yves Roger-Viollet was bending above the control panel, eyes on the window that showed the orgy going on in the chamber below. Doctor Cyrano Matelot was standing beside him. It was Matelot who saw me and shrieked.

I threw the grenade between them.

Then I threw myself flat on the floor. I was vaguely aware of a couple of women to my right who had been staring avidly through the big plate glass window that afforded a clear view into the orgy chamber. I yelled something unintelligible, to warn them.

The grenade blew up.

Shock waves hit my body, flat as it was on the floor. A woman screamed and went on screaming. I glanced up, saw the bloody figures of Yves Roger-Viollet and Cyrano Matelot—or what was left of them—scattered across half the room.

I made a leap for the control panels.

My hands went out, slammed down on levers and vari-colored buttons. Beneath me, through the control window, I saw all action stop as the men and women, freed of the radio-controlled lust that held them as slaves in its grip, fell apart and sagged to the floor, unmoving.

I turned my head. The women in here with me were alive and unharmed, though parts of their dresses had been shredded by the explosion. "Get the hell out of here!" I barked. "The police are coming in."

They turned and ran, crowding through the doorway, elbowing and clawing one another like demented animals. I felt sympathy for them. Like Margot Metayer and Sabine Bree, they were only bored, frustrated housewives seeking for thrills, thrills that HECATE offered them in return for little favors like spying on their important husbands and reporting back what they learned.

I was alone with the useless controls.

And HECATE was as good as dead.

It would be a mopping-up process now. None of the radio stimulators would work without these master controls. I felt like Abraham Lincoln must have felt after he freed the slaves.

I was still leaning over the control panels when a policeman appeared in the doorway and told me the Commissioner would see me to congratulate me on my excellent job. The police were rounding up the HECATE men and women, who were babbling and telling everything they knew to the flics. There would be scandals in high places, the officer muttered. He was obviously scandalized himself.

I followed him down the stairs.

Fourteen hours later, I was stepping out of the shower in my Plaza-Athénée suite of rooms, reaching for a shaggy towel to dry myself off. I had returned from Dampierre about four in the morning and had slept the good sleep until half an hour ago when I'd waked to take a shower.

My spirit glowed just as brightly as my skin while I worked the towel. The Commissioner had been lavish in his praise. The men and women in HECATE would be separated from their control gadgets, the French government was going to keep the affair absolutely hush-hush to prevent panic.

One by one, the operatives of HECATE would be rounded up, if they did not come forward of their own volition. They would be interrogated, their knowledge would be added to the files and information the French police already had in their possession. It would take time to sort out the entire story, to realize how deep and how far the claws of the organization had been extended. But it would be done.

HECATE itself was as dead as Yves Roger-Viollet and Cyrano Matelot. The control room was being disassembled by electronic experts. The headquarters building would be added to the hospital itself, which was being returned to the administrative control of Doctor Berlet. His daughter Noelle would help him re-establish its once untarnished reputation. Jeannette Lons was going to be named Head Nurse.

Everything was great with my world. Even Old Walrus-moustache had cabled his kudos on a job well done.

Just one thing rankled in me. Sure, call it male pride in my manhood, but I couldn't get the thought of Margot Metayer out of my head. The fiasco with her in these rooms of my suite had left psychic scars on that pride. So what if HECATE had had me under its controls? I had not performed in true Rod Damon style, and it annoyed the hell out of me.

I got dressed and went downstairs, hoping she might be sitting in the lobby. No such luck. I walked into the dining room, to fill my empty middle.

And there she was, in a lowcut cocktail gown, sipping an aperitif. She did not blink as I walked up to her table, pulled back the empty chair, and seated myself. I gestured for the waiter to set a place for me. I had the feeling she was expecting me.

"You're my guest," I told her.

I also told her over *soupe au pistou à la Provence, bouef à la mode* with carrots and onions, while finishing up with *mousse au chocolat* for dessert, and during several cups of steaming coffee exactly what had happened at the villa on Elsinore beach in Denmark. Her eyes were very wide, her lipsticked mouth a little open, as she listened.

"Two? At once?" she gasped.

I smiled. "And more than once."

"You are either a braggart or——"

"You're getting monotonous about that. Tonight I'm here to prove the truth." I grinned. "Of course, if you'd prefer to wait and talk things over with Sabine or Germaine—"

It was her turn to be amused. "They would lie, the bitches! If you had done all you claim to have done, they'd lie and say you hadn't. If you had fizzled out, they'd claim you were a humping Hercules, just to make me jealous. No, no. I much prefer to be the tester myself."

Her blue eyes challenged me across the table. I ordered Chivas Regal and toasted her loveliness. "I shall toast you in a different manner, once we're upstairs," I announced.

"Braggart! We shall see."

This time as I walked behind Madame Metayer as she walked toward the foyer archway, crowding her girdled buttocks with my loins, I reacted as if I'd been drinking the juices of the thorn apple. Standing close to her soft thigh. I let my epee nudge it. She was coloring faintly, she knew damn well I was up to par. And in the elevator, where once I hadn't so much as stirred an inch, I was now double-shanked, as the saying has it.

I caught her hand and moved it until she could play and explore if she wanted. She wanted, all right. Her fingertips measured and then double-checked, to make sure she wasn't pipe-dreaming.

She murmured, "It cannot be."

I growled, "Braggart, am I?"

Madame Metayer practically ran down the carpeted hall to my suite door. I unlocked it to let her enter first. I reached to unfasten her zipper, but she beat me to it. She had my zipper down before I knew what was happening.

"Here," she panted, moving toward a low hassock and drawing me with her with a hand on the pump handle. Yanking her skirts up to the middle of her pale white thighs so I could see her shapely stockinged legs and her garterclasps, she sat down.

Margot drew out my manhood. Her face was red with excitement as she saw its size. "A horse is no bigger," she moaned.

"The Hindus would call me *ashva,* or horse-man," I told her bowed head as she went on examining me. "Twelve fingers long, twelve fingers deep."

"What was wrong with you before?" she moaned.

"I'd just come out of a hospital," I explained, which
174

was true enough in its way. "It had a debilitating effect on me."

I knelt down, pushed her skirt back to her hips, ran my mouth and tongue along her left thigh and then the right above her stockingtops. She was moaning, trying to open and close the thighs I was caressing. She was steaming, she was one hot honeyslot, but I was the one in the control seat.

Her eyes were closed, her lips were pressed together, her head hung backward as I let my lips tell her silently that this was one evening she was never to forget. After a little while she began to tremble uncontrollably.

There was no need to wait. We had the night before us, but she was actually suffering. I hate to see a pretty woman suffer so I tilted her backward until her buttocks were on the hassock and her head was on the floor and then I took her with a savage fury that was kissing kin to rape.

Her stockinged legs came up to tighten about my trousered loins; she was fully clothed, so was I. I didn't get any extra kicks from taking her while we were dressed, it just seemed the thing to do at the time. If I could relieve her intense need, I'd be doing her a favor.

We settled into the *souak el feurdj* movement, in which my member slid in and out and right and left in a steady pulsing that I could keep up indefinitely. Under me, Margot Metayer was going crazy, screaming and wailing, clawing at my jacketed shoulders and shuddering into one orgasm after another.

"Braggart?" I whispered once.

"No, no, it is all true—if a living dream can be called true."

We went on and on, like a mechanical toy conceived in the mind of a giant toymaker. When Margot fainted dead away, I carried her to my bed and undressed her. I stripped out of my own clothes and joined her.

She woke to the caress of lips upon her nipples. She moaned, writhed her nakedness into mine and cupped the back of my neck with a hand. We kissed a long time.

"To paraphrase a famous American," I grinned, "I've only just begun to fight."

Her happy laughter was my reward as she made room

175

to take me between her thighs. While I let pleasure wash over us, I realized the rankling annoyance in my mind at my radio-controlled failure was a thing of the past. Tonight, I would prove to my satisfaction, and even more to the satisfaction of Margot Metayer, that what had happened between us some time ago was a boo-boo never to be repeated.

I must admit, she loved the way I proved it.